E. B. Borron

Report of E.B. Borron

Stipendiary Magistrate, on Part of the Basin of Hundson's Bay Belonging to

the Province of Ontario

E. B. Borron

Report of E.B. Borron
Stipendiary Magistrate, on Part of the Basin of Hundson's Bay Belonging to the Province of Ontario

ISBN/EAN: 9783337125486

Printed in Europe, USA, Canada, Australia, Japan

Cover: Foto ©Raphael Reischuk / pixelio.de

More available books at **www.hansebooks.com**

REPORT OF E. B. BORRON, ESQ.,

STIPENDIARY MAGISTRATE,

ON PART OF

THE BASIN OF HUDSON'S BAY

BELONGING TO THE

PROVINCE OF ONTARIO.

Printed by Order of the Legislative Assembly.

Toronto :

PRINTED BY GRIP PRINTING AND PUBLISHING CO., FRONT STREET.

1885.

TABLE OF CONTENTS.

COLLINGWOOD, 25th MARCH, 1885.

THE HONOURABLE O. MOWAT,
   Attorney-General, Toronto.

SIR,—I have the honour to submit herewith my Report on that part of the Provincial
Territory explored by me during the past season.

My attention has been chiefly directed to an examination of what is known as the
" Long Lake Route," from Lake Superior to James' Bay.

The object, as you are aware, was to obtain such information relative thereto, as
might aid and assist the Government in deciding upon the best mode of opening up and
developing an important section of the territory drained by the Kenogami River and its
tributaries, and at the same time of promoting and encouraging commercial intercourse
with Hudson's Bay.

It affords me much pleasure to acknowledge the obligations I am under to Dr. Bell,
of the Geological Survey of Canada, for reports, maps and tracings, showing the results of
his own exploration and surveys in this territory, which have been of the greatest
use and assistance to me throughout.

I have the honour to be, sir,

Your most obedient servant,

E. B. BORRON,
Stipendiary Magistrate.

REPORT

OF

E. B. BORRON, ESQ., STIPENDIARY MAGISTRATE,

ON

THAT PART OF THE BASIN OF HUDSON'S BAY BELONGING TO THE PROVINCE OF ONTARIO.

In the Report which I had the honour to submit of my explorations in this terri‾tory last year, I called the attention of the Government to the importance of an early opening up and development of its agricultural, timber, mineral and other resources, should the award of the arbitrators be confirmed.

I had formed a very favourable opinion of what is known as " the Long Lake route" to James' Bay, on my somewhat hurried trip over the greater part of it last year. Although late in the season, and at a period when the water in the rivers is usually low, I was alike pleased and surprised to find that from a point some fifty miles north of Long Lake to James' Bay, a distance of 250 miles, the navigation of the Kenogami and Albany Rivers was perfectly uninterrupted. Knowing that all these northern rivers, with the exception, perhaps, of Rupert's River, rise from ten to twenty feet in the spring above their summer level, I felt more than sanguine that this entire stretch would be navigable by steamers of light draught for at least six weeks after the breaking up of the ice. Having obtained the sanction of the Government, I determined to examine this route more carefully, and if possible at an earlier period in the season. Should my expectations in reference to the supposed navigable stretches on the Kenogami be realized, it was my intention to have explored for, and selected the shortest and best lines I could for the roads, which, as mentioned in last year's Report, it would be necessary to make in order to render the route complete.

It appeared to me, that I should be able to carry out this intention most effectually by proceeding inland at Michipicoten ; and from a lake called Oba, situated on the Height of Land, follow a river which has its source in that lake and flows northward. I had been told by an old Indian last year, that this river would, if followed, bring us out at Mamat‑tawa, where several large tributaries enter the Kenogami River. Mamattawa is situated about midway, in reference to that portion of the Kenogami, the navigability of which by steamers it was most important to ascertain. This route therefore promised, not only to take me more directly and speedily to this point, but also to afford me an opportunity of seeing a portion of the supposed fertile-belt in this territory which I had not hitherto been able to penetrate. Nor was it improbable that it might afford a better route to Mamat‑tawa than that by Long Lake itself.

On my arrival at Michipicoten River a great deal of time was unavoidably lost in getting our supplies and obtaining guides. Our pork, flour and biscuit, which had been forwarded from Collingwood more than ten days before by the City of Owen Sound, had not been landed, as they should, at Michipicoten, but had been carried past and left at Port Arthur. Even when I had got these things from Port Arthur, few of the Indian hunters who usually bring their furs in the spring to Michipicoten Post, had as yet arrived, and it was impossible to obtain a guide. I was under the necessity therefore of going to the Hudson Bay Company's Post at Missinaibe, not less than fifty miles out of my way, in the hope that a guide might be obtained there who knew the route from Lake Oba northward to Mamattawa. Here I was, thanks to Mr. Wilson, the officer in charge, fortunate in procuring the services of an Indian, who, although only acquainted with the route for some seventy-five or eighty miles beyond Lake Oba, was an excellent guide as far as his knowledge went, and a most admirable and trustworthy voyageur. I also procured at this post a canoe which was more suitable for our trip than one of those I had brought with me. Returning from thence to Dog Lake, the point from which I propose giving a detailed description of the route, is the station of the Canadian Pacific Railway at the north-western extremity of that lake.

From this point (which is also the headquarters of Conmee & McLennan's contract) three portages, in length about three-quarters, one-quarter and one-eighth of a mile respectively, with an intermediate pond at the end of the first, and a small lake at the end of the second portage, brought us to a large lake called Wabatonguishene. The whole distance from Dog Lake is little more than two miles in a northerly direction. The portage strikes the lake a mile or so from its southern extremity.

The Canadian Pacific Railway seemingly passes close to that end of Wabatonguishene. This lake is nearly twenty miles in length, and its width varies from a few chains to three miles. As usual, the longer axis bears north and south. It is situated at a somewhat higher level than Dog Lake, into which I am told its waters are discharged.

At the northern extremity of Wabatonguishene, we came to the Height of Land Portage, this is almost level, and about half a mile long. It runs nearly north, and terminates at a pond, the water of which flows northward down a small creek into Lake Oba. This creek is so shallow and obstructed with brush and fallen timber as to require four portages, varying from ten to fifty chains in length, in an estimated stretch of not more than four miles altogether. The fall does not appear to be more than ten or twelve feet, and the course of the creek from its source, to where it enters Lake Oba, is N.N.W.

Estimated by the eye, Lake Oba would seem to be eleven or twelve miles in length, and in few places, if any, more than one mile in width. The bearing of the longer axis is about north-north-east and south-south-west. The Oba River, which has its source in this lake, issues from its northern extremity.

A general description will be first given of this river; its navigable stretches; and the rapids, falls or other obstructions met with, as showing its importance, or otherwise, whether as a route to the North, or as facilitating the first opening up and settlement of the adjacent territory. The soil, timber and minerals will be alluded to afterwards, under their appropriate heads.

The distance from where we struck Oba Lake to its outlet is about six miles. On entering the river, we found it from one to two chains in width, and of sufficient depth to float our largest canoe. With the exception of two small rapids which were easily run by the canoes, no obstruction was met with in the first five miles. At the end of this stretch, we came to a rapid, in which the fall is six or seven feet, and here we were compelled to make a portage 250 yards in length. The portages will be numbered and referred to as 1st, 2nd, 3rd, etc., commencing with this one, as being the first, that is necessary to make in descending the river. Below this portage about four miles, a stream falls in on the west side, which my guide calls White Fish River, and comes, he says, from a large lake. The Second Portage occurs about three miles below this, or seven miles in all from the first. The fall here is seemingly about twenty feet, and length of the portage 200 yards.

Another two and a half miles, in the course of which we passed several rocky ridges and reefs, brought us to the Third Portage. It is 330 yards in length, and the fall is about 15 feet. At a point about five miles below this Third Portage and nearly twenty miles from Lake Oba, a tributary stream falls in on the right or east side, which my guide called "Coat River." Its waters also come, he says, from a good sized lake. He further informed me that from this point to Brunswick Lake, where the Hudson Bay Company formerly had a Post, is one and a half day's journey on snow-shoes. This I should take to mean about thirty or thirty five miles, a distance which agrees very closely with that shown on Dr. Bell's map (1883) to illustrate Reports of 1875, 1877, 1881.

Two miles from the junction of the Coat and Oba rivers we came to the Fourth Portage. This is 275 yards in length, and the fall is about 23 feet. There is said to be a nearer route to Lake Kabinakagami than the circuitous one afforded by following the main river. This is by a chain of small ponds with intermediate portages, the first portage beginning on the western or left bank of the Oba, about two and a half miles below the Third Portage. A little above that point I was also told one of the C. P. R. exploratory lines crossed the Oba.

Three miles below the Fourth Portage, another stream called "Gull River" falls in on the east side, and like all the others of any size in this section of the country, has its origin in one or more lakes. Eleven miles further, or say fourteen miles from the Fourth Portage, the Oba forks or divides into two branches. From Lake Oba to these forks the distance in a straight line, by Dr. Bell's map, is about twenty six miles, and the general bearing N. by E. Following the bends and turns of the river, I make the distance about thirty-five miles, which, although arrived at roughly by estimating the speed of the canoe, and noting the time required for each stretch, is, I think, tolerably correct. Two somewhat remarkable features are presented by the river at this point. If what my guide tells me be true, the two branches into which the Oba is here divided never unite again. The smaller branch, maintaining the north-easterly course, pursued by the main river up to this point, falls into the Missinaibe branch of Moose River above what are called the Albany Rapids, and is known and marked on Dr. Bell's map, as "the Albany Branch" of the Missinaibe River. The other and larger branch of the Oba turning westward, doubles back on its previous course and runs in a south-south-westerly direction, until it is within a short distance of Lake Kabinakagami, into which it discharges its water. Thus the water of the one branch ultimately reaches the coast of James' Bay at Moose Factory, and the other at Albany Factory, one hundred miles apart.* The guide, on whose truthfulness I can place the greatest reliance, tells me, that it is only one day's journey, in the spring of the year with a small canoe by this Eastern Branch, from the forks to Missinaibe River. Also, that many years ago the Hudson Bay Company had a post on Lake Kabinakagami. which was supplied with goods from Moose Factory by this route.

Following the Westerly Branch of the Oba, our progress was uninterrupted for a stretch of nearly fifteen miles, ending at a rapid in which there is a fall of about five feet ; and a portage (the Fifth), seventy-five yards in length. The greater part of this stretch was through marshes and ponds, which have no doubt formed part of Lake Kabinakagami, at a comparatively recent period. Indeed my guide says that the open water forms quite a large lake, west of the forks of the Oba. Thus, from the Fourth Portage to the forks is fourteen miles, and from the forks to the Fifth Portage is fifteen miles, making twenty-nine miles of uninterrupted canoe navigation. Five or six miles before we reached the Fifth Portage, we passed through a small lake, on the western shore of which, my guide pointed out a portage by which he said it was only a short distance to Lake Kabinakagami, but as I wished to follow the river we did not avail ourselves of it.

It was three miles and half from the Fifth Portage to where we fairly opened out into Lake Kabinakagami. This is a large lake, not less apparently than twenty miles in length, and varying seemingly from one to six miles in width. It is dotted with a number of rocky islands. I am told that there is a portage of some four or five miles in length from the south end of this lake to Lake Esnagami, the source of the Magpie branch of Michipicoten River. The Height of Land therefore passes between these two lakes, as it did between Lake Oba and Lake Wabatonguishene. Thus although the distance from Lake Oba to Lake Kabinakagami is about sixty miles, the fall in the river is really very trifling, and we still found ourselves on the plateau which forms the Height of Land, and but a short distance indeed from the water-shed. The distance from where the Oba River enters Lake Kabinakagami, to the northern extremity where it again leaves it, is about ten miles and a half. Immediately on leaving this lake the river begins to descend rapidly, again resuming the north-north-easterly course which it had held from Lake Oba to the "Big-bend or forks," before mentioned.

---

* I followed this East Branch a short distance to satisfy myself whether the current was flowing North. We could not, however, perceive much, if any, current either way, but the grass and aquatic plants seemed to bear out my guide's statement. I think it is by no means unlikely that when the water in the Oba is at or near its height in the spring, a part of the flood passes out by this branch. Whereas, later in the season, it may present every appearance of being a tributary of the Oba.

The Sixth Portage commences a little way west of the outlet and is about half a mile in length. I did not see the rapid, but my barometer indicated a fall of fifty feet. The correct fall, however, as ascertained by Dr. Bell, is thirty-three feet only. The river below Kabinakagami is hardly navigable, even by half sized canoes when loaded ; and can be of no value, either as a route to James' Bay, or as a means of opening up and developing the agricultural or other resources of the adjacent territory. I shall not therefore enter into tedious and unnecessary details in reference to the falls and rapids and portages, which it might otherwise have been desirable to give. I may simply state, that on leaving Lake Kabinakagami, the Oba River descends not less than 500 feet in the next 78 miles. This descent takes place at the falls and rapids, the current in the intervening stretches of the river being on the whole very moderate. In this distance we were obliged to make twenty-two portages, some of which were nearly a mile and a half in length. In several instances it was necessary to make portages where none (if such previously existed) could be found, and on nearly all the others more or less chopping was required to admit of the passage over them of our canoes and supplies. The necessity for this was partly owing no doubt to the want of a guide, and occasioned a great deal of delay. The guide I had obtained at Missinaibe, only knew the route from Dog Lake to a little below Lake Kabinakagami, after that we were obliged to feel our way as cautiously as possible ; I had fully expected to meet Indians, and if so intended to have hired one who knew the river and could at least show us the portages. Such portages as were visible at all seemed to be very little used, and I don't think many Indians pass up or down this river. The river is rather crooked, but the bends are generally short, and rarely more than at right angles to the general bearing or course, which from the lake to near the end of this stretch is about north-north-east by magnetic compass. This easterly bearing of the Oba led Dr. Bell, who descended it some distance below Kabinakagami, to conjecture that it might turn out to be a tributary of the Missinaibe River called the Mattawish-quai-a. It was not until we neared the end of this stretch and the river began to turn a little to the north-west, that we ourselves felt at all sure as to whether this might not be the case.

It would be desirable to have at an early date a better map of this territory than any of our present Departmental maps, which are, in reference to this territory, very incomplete and inaccurate.

Immediately below the last or Twenty-seventh Portage, which terminates the above mentioned stretch, the River Oba enters the so-called flat country underlaid by the stratified Devonian and Silurian rocks. It became in less than half a mile much wider and shallower, and at the end of a mile we arrived at a ripple or rapid upwards of a mile in length, showing sandstone in the bottom from side to side. In a short distance this was succeeded by another and much longer ripple, and on the east side of this, say two miles and a half or three miles from the portage, the sandstone appears in the bank, forming a low bluff. The great plain reposing on rocks of the Palæozoic age on which we have now fairly entered, extends, in my opinion, unbroken by hills or even elevated ridges, from this north-ward to the coast of James' Bay some 200 miles distant.

The stream exhibits the characteristic features of all the rivers I have explored in this territory, as soon as they enter this flat country. These features are, great width, extreme shallowness, and rapidity of current, in proportion to the quantity of water usually discharged. In the spring of the year, on the first melting of the snow which has been accumlating for the previous four or five months, an enormous volume of water is precipitated down these northern rivers, filling them to their fullest capacity in many places, and cutting down through the sands, clays and gravel of the overlying drift until arrested by the flat limestone or sandstone rocks which underlie the drift at a depth rarely exceeding 100 or 150 feet, and generally much less. But on the subsidence of the spring freshet, there is often barely sufficient water to cover the flat rock which for miles at a stretch forms the bed or bottom of the river. This must be the case a little later in the season at the place we have now reached. Although the water was not as yet nearly at its lowest, the depth was insufficient to float a loaded canoe. For three miles below the sand-stone bluff referred to, the voyageurs were compelled to pack nearly half our supplies on their backs and to wade the canoes over the shallow places with the remainder. Thereafter, for the next seven miles only two such demi-charges (as they are called) had to be made, the

and deeper. Some idea may be formed of the difficulty of this sort of
noes, from the fact that with strong crews of experienced voyageurs
ours to get over this stretch of ten miles. The descent from the
.o this point is very considerable; not in sudden pitches and falls
an rock as in the river above, but a strong steady descent of at least
ay 130 feet in all. The aneroid barometer indicated a much heavier
' progress had been so slow that little or no reliance could be placed
ding as they did over a period of not less than twenty-four hours.
et with fewer delays and made more satisfactory progress. Occasion-
expand to a width of from six to eight chains, and when this
ess of the water would always compel the men to get out and wade.
'iver was confined to a width of three chains or so, there was gener-
f water. In the remaining twenty miles islands are a conspicuous
er stretches of the river, the soil improves and the character of the
i trees were now noticed for the first time, and black ash were more
zer growth. The variegated sandstones and shales, so conspicuous
English River, as also on the Albany River above the forks, were
observed "in situ."
meral course of the river had turned north-westerly, I had felt con-
ould ultimately join the Kenogami River, either at or in the neigh-
iwa, where several large tributaries fall in. None of us, however,
own which of these rivers we were really descending.
when at Mamattawa last year, by the old Indian chief, that the
er had its source in a lake called Oban, or Oba, a short distance only
ource of the Michipicoten River. (See Report for 1883-84, p. 34.)
r of the water of our river was not white or muddy, but approached
at of the Negaugaming River, which also falls into the Kenogami
and was also reported to have its origin in a lake on the Height of
Michipicoten. As will be seen in that report, I had ascended the
thirty miles, and the White Water River also about six miles last
.d met with no object which we could recognize as having then seen.
r, were now soon destined to be dispelled. The appearance of the
e timber, the geological formation, and the height of the barometer,
lusion that we must be nearing Mamattawa. The water, too, although
of the White Water River at its junction with the Kenogami, was
I as we advanced. At last we came to a stream, which one of my
on, who was with me last year) pronounced to be "Fishing Creek,"
of last year's Report. This was confirmed by the junction of the Ship-
irough," River on the same (east) side, and some three or four miles
this, another mile and a half brought us to Mamattawa, and the so-
'ost of the Hudson's Bay Company, where we received a very kind and
Mr. Hunter, the officer in charge. As mentioned in last Report, p.
ll post. At this and other inland posts the Hudson's Bay Company
ipply of provisions than is absolutely necessary for the carrying on of
ies they may have a little flour or pork to spare, and at other times
nough for the officer in charge and his family. The officers and ser-
obtain their subsistence chiefly, if it be possible, from such game and
.y afford, with the aid of potatoes, patches of which are cultivated at
.ed in the territory. Under these circumstances, it was indispensable
along with us on this trip all the provisions and other supplies likely
e time we left Michipicoten until our return to Lake Superior.
e difficulties of the route, retarded our progress greatly, so much so
I left Michipicoten on the 7th of June, it was the 4th of July when
iglish River Post. I had hoped to have reached this point two
ore the spring freshet had subsided, but the unavoidable delays in
rovisions and obtaining guides at Michipicoten, disappointed me.
ng account of our journey, or voyage, from Dog Lake to Mamattawa,

it is needless almost to say that this route, by the Oba River, is of little or no value, as affording a means of opening up and developing the country in the neighbourhood of Mamattawa, much less as a route to or from James' Bay.

The distance by this route from the C.P.R. station on Dog Lake to English River Post, pursuing the bends and turns of the river, is roughly estimated as follows, viz. :—

	Distance, Miles.	Number of Portages in each stretch.
From C.P.R. station to the south end of Lake Wabatoanguishene..	2	3
" south to north end of Lake Wabatoanguishene.............	20	
" north end of Lake Wabatoanguishene to Oba Lake..........	4	5
" inlet to outlet of Lake Oba	6	
" the outlet of Lake Oba, following the Oba River, to the great south-westerly bend...............................	35½	4
" great south-westerly bend to Lake Kabinakagami	18½	1
" entrance of Oba River into Lake Kabinakagami to its outlet at north end ....,...	10½	
" outlet of Kabinakagami Lake, via Oba or Kabinakagami River, to the last or 27th portage, the commencement of the flat-rock country.....................................	78½	22
" the last or 27th portage, on the Oba River, to Mamattawa, or English River Post, the junction of the Oba, Kabinakagami, or White Water River, as also of the Negaugami River, with the Kenogami or English River.................	35	
Total estimated distance.......................	210	35

It is customary among the Indians to call rivers after the lakes in which they appear to have their source. As a result of this, however, when a river enters or expands, as it were, into a lake, the name of the river is changed to that of the last lake through which its waters pass. Thus it is that this river, on leaving Lake Oba, and until it enters Lake Kabinakagami, is known as "the Oba River," but below the latter lake as the "Kabina-kagami." Whereas, at Mamattawa, where it enters the larger Kenogami or English River, it is known as White Water River, this character of muddiness having been acquired only in the last twenty miles or so above that point. This is apt to lead to confusion, and I think it is better that a river should retain its name throughout, from its source until it either forms a junction with some larger stream, in which its waters and name are alike merged, or enters the ocean. In the case of the great lakes, into which a number of streams of nearly equal size empty, there may be good reason why the effluent river should have a distinctive name. But in this instance, the Oba is the chief, if not the only, river which enters Lake Kabinakagami, and there is no sufficient reason for changing the name on the out-flow of the waters therefrom.

I, therefore, propose to drop the other names, and call this "the Oba River," from its source in Lake Oba to Mamattawa. Again, as there are several English rivers, and notably one which is a branch of the Winnipeg River, it will be better, I think, as avoid-ing confusion, if the river which receives the water of the Oba at Mamattawa should, from its source in Kenogami or Long Lake to its junction with the Albany, be known and referred to as the Kenogami River, and not English River.

With these preliminary observations, I will now endeavour shortly to describe the principal features of the country passed through on this route, and shall speak first of the soil.

THE SOIL.

The stony, rocky, and frequently barren character of much of the country bordering on the lakes, met with on the Height of Land north of Lake Superior, is generally known The country around Dog Lake, Wabatonguishene, and Oba is apparently unsuited for agriculture, although most of it possesses a soil capable of supporting a tolerable growth of forest trees. It may well be therefore that much of this land would grow grass of a kind adapted to the soil and climate, and afford good pasture, although unfit for the production of grain. The hills in the vicinity of these lakes rise from 200 to 400 feet above the level of the water. On leaving Oba Lake, we enter on a long stretch of low, flat country, the much larger portion of which is, 1 think, swampy or marshy. For thirty-five miles below Oba Lake, only two or three low hills, and these not exceeding 100 feet in height, were seen. The fall in the river is not more, by my reckoning, than about two feet in a mile. On the flats, I found in some places a considerable thickness of black swamp muck reposing on a clay loam. These, where sufficiently high above water, would make good meadows. On the higher and drier banks and ridges the soil is generally sandy or gravelly and light. Below what I have called the Big Bend, where the Oba doubles back on its previous north-easterly course, for nearly fifteen miles, the route runs through marsh and lake nearly the whole way, until we enter an arm of Lake Kabinakagami. Higher hills once more come in view a little below the Big Bend, partially surrounding what appears to have been at one time a very extensive lake. Grass and willows grow luxuriantly on the drier parts of these marshes. That portion of the eastern side of Kabinakagami Lake which I had any opportunity of seeing, was sandy and unarable, and the northern end at and near the portage very broken and rocky. In the first stretch of six or seven miles below Lake Kabinakagami, some tracts of very fair land were seen on both sides of the river, but much of that on the immediate banks is low. From this to the sixteenth mile below Kabinakagami Lake, or say to the 11th Portage, the banks are higher, but the soil is generally light and sandy, though occasionally areas of better land were met with. In the next ten miles, terminating at the 14th Portage, the frequency of sand banks on alternate sides of the river, and from twenty to one hundred feet in height, indicates a sandy soil, and a somewhat rolling country, which, if seeded down to grass, would in all probability afford reasonably good pasture. Where river bottoms occur the soil is richer, being more loamy in its nature. In this sand, fragments and pebbles of the Laurentian, Huronian and Devonian rocks are more or less common, and where, as on the top and slopes of the ridges, the sand has been washed down by rain or otherwise, the number of these larger fragments seen on the surface is greater in proportion, and imparts a gravelly appearance to the soil.

In the next stretch, say from the 14th to the 20th Portage, a distance by the windings of the river of about twenty miles, the surface soil, although still sandy or gravelly, is evidently underlaid by clay, which appears to rise nearer to the surface as we proceed north, until at end of this stretch, a little below the 20th Portage, I found what appeared to me the drift clay at the surface. It is probable that, at some little distance back from the river, this clay reaches to and forms more or less of the surface soil. The character of the country is still rolling, and capable, in my opinion, of being converted into good grass and pasture land. The lower and richer, but frequently wet and swampy land, would form in many places fine meadows. From the 20th to the 21st Portage, a stretch of eighteen miles, the land is lower in the vicinity of the river, with a larger proportion that may be called swampy. In a number of places, however, ridges or banks occur, which were forty or fifty feet in height, and I am of opinion that the general elevation of the flat country we here pass through is not less than that height above the river, and that the low swampy belt is chiefly alluvial land formed by the river. At one point, where I landed and went back a short distance, I found that, although the soil appeared to be sandy on the river bank, yet on attaining the level plateau, and proceeding inland two hundred and fifty or three hundred yards, the soil was a clay loam, covered with such a depth of sphagnum moss that it was almost ice cold ; and the timber, which had been of good size on the river bank, was in consequence stunted and unhealthy. It is exceedingly probable, although we had not as yet actually arrived at the point where the country reposes on the Silurian and Devonian rocks, that the drift clays have already become general, if not universal, and wherever the surface is flat, it will be found wet, cold, and covered to a greater or less depth with sphagnum moss and peat a short distance only from the banks of the river and its tributaries.

In the next fifteen miles, rock (which was very rarely seen last stretch) is much more frequently met with, in the form of low reefs of Laurentian gneiss and syenite, which, crossing the river in an easterly and westerly direction, occasioned numerous rapids and falls.

The descent in this stretch of fifteen miles only is not less, I think, than 200 feet, and it necessitated, as I have already stated, the making of six Portages, or from No. 22 to No. 27 inclusive. The land in the vicinity of the river is here more stony and broken than it has been at any time since we left the first Portage below Kabinakagami Lake.

Still the reefs seem to extend a very short distance on either side before they are entirely covered by the drift, and my belief is that a mile from the river and its branches the area of actual rock surface is not five per cent. of the whole territory passed through, from Lake Kabinakagami to the end of this stretch.

The land, owing to its broken character, is drier and less swampy on this stretch; and where not too rough with boulders will afford good pasture, and more limited areas capable of growing root and even grain crops. The soil is more or less loamy, and abounds with calcareous matter, the debris of the limestone beds to the north.

It is at the foot of this, the 27th and last Portage on the Oba River, that we fairly enter upon the flat country, underlying which we have stratified beds of limestone, sandstone and shale of the Devonian and Silurian series. These rocks extend unbroken, and, I believe, at no great depth below the surface, from this point to the coast of James' Bay. The general character of the surface of this great plain is similar to that which it presents on the Abittibi River, and the Mattagami and Missinaibe branches of Moose River, below what are known as "the Long Portages." As stated in former reports, by far the greater part of the surface of this plain is covered with peat mosses and bogs, called Muskegs by the natives, and in some places with what may be termed morasses, shallow ponds and lakes. The arable land is confined to the immediate banks of the rivers, which act as drains to a certain extent. The flatness of the country, however, and clayey character of the soil or subsoil, limits the natural drainage to a narrow strip or belt on each side of the principal rivers and their tributaries.

From the last portage to the junction of the Oba and Kenogami Rivers at Mamattawa, is roughly estimated at thirty-five miles. The alluvial soil, whether on the flats and banks of the river or on the islands, is almost always good, being a sandy loam, rich in calcareous matter.

Of such land, however, there does not seem to be a great deal for the first fifteen miles; but in the last stretch of twenty miles the alluvial flats and points were more frequent, and appeared to increase in number and extent, if not in fertility also, as we approached Mamattawa.

At Mamattawa, the soil, as seen at the Hudson Bay Company's post, is remarkably good; and on the banks of the Kenogami, the Negaugami and Oba Rivers, all of which meet at that point, there is room, I believe, for a fine settlement.

TIMBER.

In the territory north of the Height of Land and south of James' Bay, there is, in my opinion, a very small proportion of the surface not actually covered by water, that cannot be rendered fit for the growth of forest trees of more or less value. The adaptation of the soil and climate is unquestionable, for we find good sized and healthy trees of various kinds, wherever the other conditions of growth are in any degree favourable. The other conditions which are in my opinion the most important factors in limiting the growth of forests in this territory, are chiefly two, insufficient drainage and the too frequent recurrence of bush-fires.

It is well to know, however, in a question of so much importance, that these conditions are the ones most amenable to our influence.

As regards the imperfect natural drainage of a very large portion of this territory, and its causes, I need only refer to my Report for 1880, pp. 6, 8 and 9. Admitting that the drainage of a very large proportion of the great plain to the south of James' Bay is too imperfect to allow a natural or spontaneous growth of healthy timber of any kind, I do not know any country where such vast tracts of land can be so easily drained and fitted for the growth of timber and grass, if not also of roots and grain, as in

ıatural condition the clay soil, which largely predominates, becomes
'e the immediate banks of the rivers. This wetness favours the
hagnum), which, increasing in thickness as we retire still further
fs, and at last kills the timber.
and ultimate destruction of the timber is owing chiefly I think to
follow from the growth and increasing thickness of the bog-moss.
luces a constant and permanent state of wetness. The inclination
ain is generally such as would ensure the running off of the water, if
l unencumbered with decayed vegetable matter, or a living vegetable
' this bog-moss. There are few parts where there is not a fall of at
le, and the general height of the surface above the numerous rivers
ed, is rarely less than thirty or forty feet and frequently as much as
ıt the effect of the accumulation to the depth of only a foot or
s and peat, is to so hinder the running away of the water, that the
ıaked, so to speak, with moisture, a condition very unfavourable to
inds of forest trees.
ct that such a covering of moss and peaty matter keeps the
nderlying soil extremely low during the whole of the summer
ıtible with the growth of any healthy or valuable timber. I
r such circumstances, found the ground frozen in the month of
lly ever known the temperature to exceed forty degrees (or eight
e freezing point) at any period of the summer or autumn. The
far to seek. In the first place, the evaporation which goes
·ered with this wet sponge-like bog-moss, must have a tendency
ture, precisely as water, in India and other countries, is cooled in
ɛstic use. lly far the greater portion of the solar heat is thus, I
ı the vapour. Of that which remains another moiety is lost by
liation," which from such a surface is no doubt excessive. Finally,
ater from below, the lower stratum, becoming warmer and lighter,
laced by the cooler water from above, a series of currents, upwards
tablished, and the heat quickly diffused throughout the whole mass,
.es from above and falls on a surface of still water, no such motion
is only by "conduction," as in the case of solid bodies, that the
it can be transmitted downwards. Where the water is gathered
·arely or ever is absolutely still, owing to the disturbances and
the wind, and consequently the heat is distributed, if not equally,
derable depth. But in the case of these peat mosses or muskegs,
of the swamps and marshes,) which cover so many thousand square
', the water, unaffected by the wind and thickened with peat and
most motionless and stagnant. In this condition it is doubtless
ductors" of heat known, nor is the conducting power of sphagnum
her than that of the water. The solar heat thus penetrates the
ant depth, and I think it is rather owing to the influence of warm
cause that these muskegs, at a depth of two or three feet from
itinue frozen all the year round. Few persons who have tramped
amps, and even marshes, and occasionally sunk through to their
observed, without the aid of a thermometer, the icy coolness of
circumstances.
d, if the soil be well-drained the solar heat penetrates to a very
d is stored up as it were, to be given off in winter. When the
tion of these wide-spreading muskegs shall have been completed,
evoted to the growth of timber, of grass, or of grain, the effect on
ıole territory cannot be otherwise than beneficial in the highest
ll sooner or later be reclaimed, I have not the shadow of a doubt.
territory situated between the Height of Land and the flat or
erred to, is of a more broken and rolling character, and although
·s and swamps, and even some peat mosses in this belt, the land is,
ier, and generally supports a growth of some kind of timber. It is,

however, in this region that bush-fires are most frequent and destru
from Lake Oba to the 27th Portage, four-fifths of the country, in
over-run by fires within the last thirty or forty years. I am incline
invention of " friction matches," and their universal use by the nat
least, ascribed the frequency of bush-fires in recent times. Fires ar
for warmth or for the cooking of food, but on almost every occasion
or boy stops, if it be only to rest or smoke, the chances are he
leaves and sticks together and make what is called a smudge to keep
be water convenient, it is just possible he may extinguish it whe
water is at hand he most likely leaves it to spread or not, as circu
or otherwise. As flies are most numerous and troublesome during t
season of the year, many bush-fires have doubtless been thus oc
too, have in all probability been started by explorers for minerals,
and although these fires have generally commenced on or near the
Superior or Huron, they have extended their ravages in many insta
the Height of Land. I noticed this season the smoke of nume
Height of Land, which had doubtless originated in want of care c
engaged in clearing the line for the Canadian Pacific Railway.

The principal forest trees met with on the Oba, are spruce,
balsam, on the low flats and river bottoms. Aspen and white bir:
banks and ridges, and Banksian pine on the poorer sands. Cedar wa
especially at or near the rapids. I noticed no white pine north of
but saw some very fair red pine on the east side of Lake Kabina
trees measured in some instances as much as eighty inches in circu
tamarac fifty inches, poplar sixty, aspen fifty, birch forty-eight and
As we neared Mamattawa, black ash and elm trees of large size w
black ash were noticed at short intervals throughout, but no elm.
English River Post measured as much as nine feet in circumference.
are the most valuable timbers on the Oba. At one place where
below the twentieth Portage, I counted eight spruce trees measu:
inches to eighty inches circumference at the butt, growing on littl
chain of land. This, however, was exceptional, and confined in a
immediate bank of the river.

I am thoroughly persuaded that at a moderate expense for dra
attention to thinning out, and to the prevention of fires, vast forest
canoe-birch and aspen, can be grown in this territory. Probably a:
of the territory belonging to Ontario north of the Height of Lanc
and white pine.

There is an impression abroad that the plateau which forms th
the north, is so elevated that hardly anything will grow. This is
this Height of Land plateau is little higher in point of fact than th
Georgian Bay from Lake Ontario.

MINERALS.

From Oba Lake to the last or Twenty-seventh Portage, descendi:
at the rapids, and not always even at these, that the rock is seen i:
with, it always consisted of hard crystalline, non-fossiliferous rocl
Metamorphic. Among them, gneiss, syenite, micaceous and hornble
most conspicuous. The veins were neither numerous or promisi:
examined appear to contain any mineral or metal of economic value
Twenty-seventh Portage we came, as already mentioned, to the out cro
Devonian rocks. As we continued our course down the river, I obse
tions of iron, and nine or ten miles from the portage, I found consi:
carbonate or clay-iron ore, associated with brown hematite ore. Tl
form beds, but were so situated that I was unable to ascertain thei
no doubt however that iron ores of this description can be readily ob

unlimited quantities, at and near theout-crop of these formations. They are met with under almost precisely the same circumstances, on the Mattagami Branch of Moose River, and are accompanied by the same ochres and clays. I have noticed strong indications of these ores also on the Kenogami or English River, and in a lesser degree on the Albany and Abittibi Rivers. These ores and clays will in my opinion be found abundantly over a wide extent of this territory, and when it is opened up, cannot fail I believe to prove valuable, associated as they are with inexhaustible beds of peat, and with more or less lignite coal.

KENOGAMI RIVER.

Under the head "Opening up the Country," in last year's report, pp. 66, 67 and 68, I stated, " that, having due regard to efficiency and economy, the conclusion I had arrived at was, that in the absence of direct railway communication, which is not likely to be available for many years, the best route to the fertile belt described in that report, as well as to James' Bay, was by Long Lake.

The route there alluded to, the greater part of which I had passed hurriedly over that season, was as follows :

	Miles.
From Jackfish Bay, Lake Superior, to Long Lake, by road (which it was suggested that the Province should make)	22
" the south end of Long Lake to the First Portage on the Kenogami River (unbroken navigation)	58
" First Portage to the Eighteenth or last Portage on the Kenogami River, by road (which it was also proposed should be made by the Province)....	45
" the foot of the Eighteenth Portage on the Kenogami to Albany Factory, James' Bay (believed to afford unbroken steam navigation for six weeks in the spring)	250
In all	375

Of which 308 miles would be navigable water, and 67 miles colonization roads.

That part of the long navigable stretch on the Kenogami and Albany Rivers, in regard to which I had any doubt, was the stretch of sixty miles from the Eighteenth Portage on the Kenogami to Mamattawa.

I had started from the Eighteenth Portage at noon of the 23rd of July last year (1883), and in a large and somewhat heavily laden canoe, reached with ease the Hudson Bay Company's Post at Mamattawa about six o'clock the following evening. Nor did we, so far as I can remember, get once aground in this whole stretch of sixty miles. As the river had been open for at least two months at that time, this fact augured well, as it seemed to me, for the navigability of this part of the river by steamers of light draught, earlier in the season, before the subsidence of the spring freshet.

One object of this year's explorations was to re-examine more carefully this stretch, and also that between Mamattawa and the Albany River, and thus ascertain with certainty as to the navigability of the Kenogami.

My desire was to have reached Mamattawa not later than the middle of June, or some four or five weeks earlier than last year.

Delays, however, alike unexpected and unavoidable at Michipicoten and upon the journey, as already mentioned, prevented my reaching this starting point for my survey of the Kenogami River, before the fourth of July.

On my arrival I divided my party, Mr. A. Stephen being detailed with three men to go down to "the Forks " or junction of the Kenogami and Albany Rivers, some sixty miles below Mattawa, to take soundings and obtain such other information as he could in reference to the navigation—while I myself ascended the river and re-examined the upper sixty-mile stretch, from Mamattawa to the first obstruction to canoe navigation, namely, " the Eighteenth Portage " from Long Lake.

Starting out we passed the junctions of the Oba and the Negaugami, both of which supply large quantities of water. It was not until we had ascended the Kenogami a short

2 (B. R.)

distance above the junction of the Negaugami, that it became evident the water in upper Kenogami was really much less in quantity than it had been when we had pas down (nearly three weeks later) last year. I cannot account for this in any other than that the snow-fall had been heavier over the basin drained by the Kenogami dur the winter of 1882-83 than that of 1883-84, or that the spring was colder and later in former than the latter year.

From enquiries which I made, I think it is partly owing to both these causes, but chi to the lightness of the snow-fall last winter. Be that as it may, however, the increa shallowness of the water became more and more apparent as we advanced. The rive fairly navigable for the first seven miles, only two places having been met with in distance where the water did not considerably exceed two feet in depth ; with the clea evidence afforded by the marks on the banks and trees, that the river had been from to twelve feet higher earlier in the season. It was noticeable however, that the grea rise had been in that part of the river below the junction of the Negaugami. In stretch we had met with no solid rock in the bottom, and the breadth of the river not therefore out of all proportion to the depth and quantity of water.

Above this point, the stratified rocks of the Palæozoic Age approach the surface thereafter for fifty-three miles, at short intervals, form the bottom or bed of the rive all its longer reaches.

In these reaches the downward course of the river generally corresponds with dip of the sandstones, limestones and shales which form its bed. As already stated in description of the Oba, this river under like circumstances expands to an e: ordinary width, and the depth is diminished in an inverse ratio thereto. In the depth is diminished to a greater extent than can be attributed to the incre breadth alone of the river, and is partly due to the greater rapidity of the current.

The water may be best described as flowing in a broad thin sheet over a flat bottom of such general uniformity that, although the river may be upwards of hundred yards in width, and the water not two feet deep at any point, the bed-rock nowhere appear above the surface, but is covered by the water from side to side.

Such a bottom is not favourable to the formation of channels, and consequentl such channels have been formed in the flat bed-rocks of limestone or sandstone. On other hand, it is often pitted with holes left by portions of the bed rock which have torn up and carried away, in all probability by the ice. Of course such holes a no advantage as respects the navigation. These cavities, however, if more a foot in depth below the general surface of the bed rock, are usually mor less filled with loose angular pieces of the rock itself which have been brought dow the current. One effect of this pitted and ragged condition of the bottom, combined a gradual but at the same time a very considerable descent, is the production of whe called "ripples" in the river, stretches of greater or less length in which the wa jumping and boiling with much energy and noise from bank to bank, but nevert shallow, and unaccompanied by the formidable chutes, the heavy swells and whirlpool with in the rapids, occasioned by the reefs of Laurentian or metamorphic rocks in the section of this and other rivers. When flooded the water flows in a strong, stead almost smooth current over most of these stretches, the inequalities in the bottom are sufficient to occasion ripples when the water is shallow, producing very little di ance on the surface when deeper. Between these broad shallow reaches we freqt found from four to six feet of water, but on the reaches themselves the depth gen ranged from one to two feet only. Notwithstanding the shallowness of these porti the river, and the great difficulty experienced in ascending this sixty miles, even in c my confidence in its navigability, earlier in the season, would not have been greatly sha there had been satisfactory evidence, that while the spring freshet lasted, the water ha at a much higher level. But while the lower Kenogami rises ten or twelve feet, and po of the upper Kenogami from six to eight feet, the high water marks of last spring's fi as seen on some of the broadest and shallowest reaches, were in several instances barely feet higher than the then level of the water. Thus the depth of the water on these r when the flood was at its greatest height this spring could not have exceeded fou Still I see no reason why, such steamers as are employed on the western and north-w vers, of light draught and considerable power, should not be able to make a few trips as up as the Portage about the time that the spring freshet is at its height.

In the lower sixty mile stretch of the Kenogami, commencing at Mamattawa and terminating at its junction with the Albany River, Mr. Stephen found only five places here the water was of less depth than four feet, and of these only one that did not exceed to feet. As the water rises in this section of the river all of ten feet during the spring ishet, there should certainly be no difficulty in navigating this stretch, for at all events weeks in the months of May and June, and again probably for a short time in the month of October.

From the " Forks " or the junction of the Albany and Kenogami Rivers to Albany ctory, James' Bay, is fron 120 to 130 miles. I passed up the Albany River to its source 1881, and down this particular section of it in 1883. On both occasions this happened be in the month of August when the water in these northern rivers is usually at its vest ebb. The banks everywhere, however, afford abundant evidence of the depth of water in the spring and early summer. The boats of the Hudson's Bay Company, loaded th supplies for English River Post (Mamattawa), Marten's Falls, Osnaburgh, and formerly en Lac Seul, have regularly passed up and down this stretch of the Albany River with- being obliged, as I understand, to make any portages. Some of these boats carry five is and draw two feet of water when loaded. That belonging to English River Post was ay on its second trip when I arrived. It returned before Mr. Stephen and the men raged in the examination of the lower stretch of the Kenogami left English River Post join me. I ascertained from them that even at this season no difficulty further than t always occasioned by the strength of the current had been experienced by the boat- n, and that the voyage from Albany Factory, about 190 miles, had been accomplished nine days.

As the result of my own observations and enquiries, I have little or no doubt that s portion of the lower Albany can be navigated by steamers for nearly the same length time as the lower stretch of the Kenogami River.

Having ascertained this much in reference to the navigation of the Kenogami and any rivers, it became necessary on our arrival at the First Portage ascending (or hteenth descending) to decide whether or not it was still desirable to make the sug- ted colonization road from Long Lake to this point. For reasons that will be fully ed hereafter, but more particularly in view of the very short period that the upper nogami is navigable, it appeared to me that it would not be advisable to make this d for some time, if at all.

I concluded therefore to push on to Long Lake by the river, making such general ervations and enquiries by the way as might enable me to give an opinion as to the cticability of making the road should its construction be determined upon at any ure period.

This I did, and the conclusion I have arrived at is, that when the progress of settle- t renders this road necessary it can be easily made, the character of the country being gether favourable.

On our arrival at the Hudson's Bay Company's Post at Long Lake, I had expected ave found there some provisions that were to have been forwarded from Pic. The er in charge of this post had left home for Lake Superior on business, and with him gone nearly all the Indians, the object of the latter being to receive their annuity. stores were locked up, and the two men left to take care of the place knew nothing of flour. However, this was of little consequence as we had enough to last us until we d reach Lake Superior. It was a greater disappointment being again unable to procure nide to Lake Superior via Black River.

As preliminary and absolutely essential to any settlement of the country between Long e and Mamattawa, a road from Lake Superior or from the Canadian Pacific Railway to g Lake will be indispensable. The construction of such a road from Jackfish Bay to south end of Long Lake was suggested in my last Report, p. 67. I was desirous efore of following a route sometimes said to be taken by the Indians in small canoes n Black River, in order that I might see the country and be able to form an opinion o the possiibility of making such a road.

Having obtained all the information we could from the Indians at the Post
cluded to at least make an attempt to find our way, the whole distance from Lon
to Lake Superior being only some twenty-two miles in a direct line, according to t
mate of Dr. Bell. Leaving Long Lake House, we arrived at the southern extre
the lake, some fifty-two miles distant, early on the third day. This lake havi
carefully explored and reported upon by Dr. Bell of the Geological Survey, and
any lengthened description of it on my part is uncalled for, Dr. Bell's report bein
correct so far as I have had an opportunity of verifying it. I would merely say, s
the navigation is concerned it leaves nothing to be desired; it is navigable fron
end, and is one of the finest natural canals I have ever seen. Like almost all the
or near the Height of Land, the trough which its water fills is in my opinion of
origin, and has formed one of the channels along which an ice current or river ha
source in the great Arctic Glacier or "Ice-Cap," has forced its way over the H
Land during what is known as the Glacial Period. The ruins of the softer P
strata in the north over which this ice-current has passed are scattered all al
route from where they are "in situ" on the Kenogami River, to the shores
Superior. The most remarkable of these is a calcareous sand, light-coloured and
ingly fine. It makes its first appearance on the shores of Long Lake, and formi
does, white banks from twenty to one hundred feet in height, is very conspicuo
singular sand is met with at intervals from thence down the valley of the Blac
almost if not quite to the shores of Lake Superior. A sample taken from a l
more than five or six miles from the mouth of Black River, yielded twenty-five
of carbonate of lime, and I think some of those from Long Lake which I was no
bring along with me, and have not yet received, will be found upon examinatio
tain a still larger proportion of calcareous matter.

FROM LONG LAKE TO LAKE SUPERIOR.

At the south end of Long Lake we found what I believed to be the first o
of Portages, separated by little ponds and lakes, which the Indians had told us
be necessary to traverse. The bad condition in which this portage was, satisfie
in order to reach Lake Superior by this route in a reasonable time, it would be
to leave our largest canoe and almost everything else, not absolutely indi
Taking with us therefore our clothes, camp equipage and provisions for six days
rest of our things, inclusive of the Geological and Mineral specimens I had colle
"cached" at this point.
The First Portage commences at the most southerly point of Long Lake
small brook almost dry at this season, enters the Lake. It ascends this brook
two hundred yards and ends at a marshy pond. There is but little rise and tl
is south-westerly. A good deal of chopping and underbrushing was needed to
portage passable.
Embarking on this pond which is partly formed by an old beaver dam, w
to make about half a mile, partly pond, partly a sluggish creek. This soon
obstructed with drift wood, that we were compelled to make another, the Seco
300 yards long and running about south. Here also much chopping of fallen
necessary. This Portage terminated like the last at a beaver dam, above whicl
another pond. This was partly open water, partly marsh, and terminated in i
be called a beaver meadow. Here we were at fault and obliged to camp.
search on the part of my voyageurs, failed to discover the next Portage that
next day one of the oldest and most experienced hunters, found very faint sig
might have been at one time a Portage, to the east of the marsh referred to
this up for nearly a mile, we at length came to a small lake, where his conjec
confirmed. Bush fires had over-run the whole of this part of the country, see
or fifteen years ago. The timber, most of which was only killed by the fire
wards been blown down by the wind. The trunks lay crossing each other ir
ceivable direction, with a second growth coming up between. This so obl

s of a Portage, that it was a matter of surprise to me that
t up and follow it out. It took all that remained of the
d render it passable.
e upper end of the Second Portage, we proceeded across the
ly direction as far as we could get in the canoe, or say about
g on the east side we proceeded to cross this Third Portage.
sses over dry gravelly soil the whole way. It rises thirty or
ppears to descend as much if not more on the other. This is
of Land Portage. The water which escaped over the beaver
ing into Hudson's Bay, and that from the small lake at the
scending into Lake Superior. The low ground of the marsh
l to, sweeps round on the right or west side of the Portage,
e one if not two small ponds, between that at which the Port-
where it terminates. One at least of these ponds discharges its
ild not be at all surprised if in the spring it was possible to
Long Lake to this the source of the Black River without any
as might be required to cross the beaver dams. The real
nd cannot be more than a very few feet above the high water
t the hollow or depression which this route follows is in my
on of the Glacial trough which forms Long Lake itself.
at the end of the Third Portage we passed in the next three
: or seven small lakes. In this stretch we were obliged to
fhe 4th was 1½ chains only in length, the 5th was 24 chains,
d the 7th was 14 chains in length. These Portages were
med to me, rather by the insufficient quantity of water in the
the greatness of the fall, which up to this point has not been
y through a lake, brought us to the Eighth Portage, about ten
had the first fall (30 feet) worthy of particular notice. The
his Portage, with the exception of one or two short stretches
l from south-westerly to south-easterly, and is on the whole
th.
one-eighth of a mile on a south-south-westerly course brought
out 5 chains in length with a fall of three feet. Below this
ied, again on a south-south-westerly course, and in quarter of
as reached. This Portage is about 16 chains in length. A
quarter of a mile in length across another lake, brought us to
yards long, in a south-south-easterly direction. From this to
more over a lake, the distance being half a mile and the
a Portage is 250 yards in length and runs about south-south-
a larger lake than any we had met with since Long Lake.
itimated from Long Lake to this point is nearly eight miles.
in this, most of the Portages were owing rather to the shallow-
wood or boulders of the streams connecting the various lakes
idden or great fall. In making these Portages we frequently
inks of the river, and I was not always therefore in a position
bable amount of the fall. Small aneroid barometers are un-
'nce goes, where the fall is under 50 feet. From the generally
ges, however, I am persuaded that with the exception of the
fall was 30 feet) the descent at the other four Portages does
. Allowing 20 feet for fall between the Third or Height of
Portage, the total fall from the Height of Land Portage to this
iut 100 feet, or twelve and a half feet per mile. From the
'ortage our course was south-south-easterly for quarter of a
rly for about one mile. The breadth of the lake was about
illowness of a narrow channel then compelled us to make a
th) two chains in length. The width of the lake in some
as from half a mile to three quarters of a mile. For the first

two miles our course was again south-south-westerly, and for the next three quarters of
mile about south. This brought us to the end of the lake, the total length of which w;
thus about four miles, with a longitudinal bearing of nearly south-south-west. The riv
at the outlet of this lake is no doubt a good sized stream with ample depth of water
float a loaded canoe earlier in the season, but we now found it so shallow that all han
had not only to get out and walk, but in many places the men had to pack more or le
of the baggage on their backs, in order to lighten the canoes. As in addition to this v
had to wade most of the time, our progress was neither satisfactory nor agreeable. The
is a strong and steady fall in this stretch of river the length of which is three miles, a
average course south-east. Following after this there is a still water stretch, partly riv
and partly small ponds, about five-eighths of a mile in length, course south-south-east. Th
brought us to a lake one and a quarter miles in length, and bearing east-south-east. C
the river about five chains below this lake we came to where there was a fall of 12 fee
which compelled us to make the Fourteenth Portage. This was 8 chains in length a;
the bearing of it also was east-south-east. In the short distance of 150 yards we came
the Fifteenth Portage 220 yards in length, with a fall of 20 feet.

The bearing of this Portage is south-south-east. The distance from Long Lake
this Fifteenth Portage is thus estimated at a little over seventeen miles. The fall to t.
Twelfth Portage inclusive was roughly calculated at 100 feet. Adding to this 32 feet f
the fall in the Fourteenth and Fifteenth Portages, and 28 feet for the fall in oth
stretches, the total descent will be about 160 feet.

From this Fifteenth Portage to the Sixteenth, which is within a mile of La
Superior, no sudden falls or violent rapids occur in the river requiring Portages to
made. But there is notwithstanding a very considerable though gradual descent near
the whole way. This is probably as much as 8 feet per mile. The distance, following t
river, is roughly estimated at 15 miles, and the fall in this stretch at about 120 feet. T
total distance from Long Lake to the last or Sixteenth Portage will thus be about
miles, and the total fall about 280 feet.

The only sudden drop in the river or in the surface itself from Long Lake to La
Superior, is in the last half mile, where it amounts to not less than 150 feet. The porta
(Sixteenth) takes off about half a mile above the falls, at the mouth of the Black Riv
and about the same distance below the crossing of the C. P. R., and is a good mile
length to Lake Superior. The fall, as above stated, is not less than 150 feet or more th
one-half of that in the previous 32 miles.

The exceedingly crooked character of Black River in its lower stretches may be inferr
from the fact that no fewer than 111 compass bearings had to be taken in the last
miles in order to arrive at an approximate estimate of its course.

The following are the general courses taken on this route, with the lengths and fal

	Course.	Distance, miles.	Fall, feet.
From south end of Long Lake to the Twelfth Portage, inclusive...................	S. by W.	12	100
From Twelfth Portage to river on east side, supposed to come from Trout Lake, and including the Thirteenth, Fourteenth and Fifteenth Portages.......	S. E.	6¾	74
From Trout Lake River to beginning of S. W. stretch...............................	S.	1¾	14
From beginning of S. W. stretch to beginning of S. S. E.............................	S. W.	6½	52
From beginning of S. S. E. stretch to Sixteenth Portage.............................	S. S. E.	5	40
From beginning of Sixteenth Portage to Lake Superior.............................	S. E.	1	150
		33	430

Both distances and falls are estimated for the most part by the eye, and are only
'ed, in the absence of a regular instrumental survey, as a rough approximation. The
I distance of 33 miles from Long Lake to Lake Superior is the length of the route
,wing all the turns and bends of the rivers and lakes. The distance in a straight line
lot be so much by five or six miles at the very least, and is no doubt still shorter to
:fish Bay. The distance from Jackfish Bay to the south end of Long Lake has been
nated at about 22 miles only, and I am persuaded that a direct line from the extreme
h end of Jackfish Bay to Long Lake will not in all probability exceed that estimate.
Having been informed on my arrival at Jackfish Bay that the validity of "the Award"
not been sustained by the Privy Council, I considered, in view of the whole circum-
ces, that there was little or nothing to be gained by returning to Long Lake, as I had
rwise intended. To have returned with loaded canoes by Black River in the then low
lition of the water, would have been all but impossible, and to have returned by Pic
er route involved a circuit of nearly 200 miles. In addition to this, reports of riots
bloodshed at Michipicoten had reached the ears of my voyageurs, and they were so
ious about their families that I doubt if any of the men from that place could have been
iced to remain. I concluded therefore that it would be best to pay them off, and
r no further expense in carrying on these explorations until circumstances were on the
le more favourable.

ROADS.

The roads, the construction of which I suggested in last year's report, pp. 67, 68
69, were intended to serve a three-fold object : Firstly, the opening up of the country
gricultural settlement ; secondly, the development of the mineral and timber resources
he territory north of the Height of Land ; and thirdly, the encouragement and pro-
ion of trade and commerce between our Province and the region bordering on Hud-
s Bay. In the absence of railway communication, the route by way of Long Lake,
ully described in that report, appeared to me to offer greater advantages than any
:r.
After the examination now made, with this special object in view, I still remain of
opinion that, so far as common roads and more or less navigable water stretches can
1 a good and desirable means of travel and transport, this route is much superior to
other known to me. It can be made at much less cost, and will accomplish some of
objects in view more fully and completely. But this said, I am constrained to admit
, the advantages in respect of other of these objects which it was expected to secure
lot be fully realized, on account of the imperfect navigation of the Upper Kenogami
the shortness of the period during which it is available. A waggon road could be
.e without difficulty, and at a very moderate expense, from Lake Superior to Long
e, and from Long Lake to the last portage on the Kenogami. Throwing off the fall of
feet in the last mile of Black River, or starting, as it were, from the top of the bank
Jake Superior ; and assuming the distance, in a moderately straight line up the Black
er valley, to be twenty-six or twenty-seven miles to Long Lake, it will be seen that
rise or inclination is not more than twelve feet per mile. It will be seen, too, from
foregoing description of this route, that this rise is very gradual. The soil is dry and
rally sandy or gravelly, and although the valley is sometimes so hemmed in as to be
e more than a gorge, there appeared to be always (with one or two trifling exceptions)
u for a road without the necessity of having recourse to rock-cutting. A good line
road can unquestionably be got up Black River valley, from the Canadian Pacific
lway bridge or crossing to Long Lake, and a still shorter line might in all probability
ocated from the extreme north end of Jackfish Bay, and passing between Trout Lake
Owl Lake to Long Lake.
The next link in this route is Long Lake itself, the navigation of which, from its
hern extremity to the first rapid on the Kenogami, some fifty-eight miles, is quite
:ticable for boats drawing three feet of water. Were it not for a sand-bar at the
et, double that draught could be carried through between the points named.
From the First to the Eighteenth or last Portage on the Kenogami, the distance by

the river does not exceed fifty miles, and the fall is, I believe, about 400 feet. As it is not navigable, it was proposed to build a road around this part of the river, the length of which was not expected to exceed forty-five miles. From this year's explorations, and the information which I have been able to obtain otherwise, I am convinced that a very good route for it can be found. The country a few miles south-east of the river is, I believe, dry and otherwise exceedingly favourable. Near the river it is, on the other hand, not unfrequently marshy or swampy, and the expense of making a road would be greater. The length of this road, from the First to the Eighteenth Portage below Long Lake, will not in any case exceed forty-five miles, and if not obliged to diverge too far from a straight line it should be less.

That the construction of the road from Lake Superior to Long Lake must precede anything like systematic settlement of the territory north of Long Lake is unquestionable. And further : as settlement advances it will be undoubtedly necessary to make the other road above referred to. But in view of the very short period that the Upper Kenogami would seem to be navigable, and the inadequacy of the route, even if completed, to serve the other important objects that were contemplated, it would be no more than prudent to let the matter stand over for the present, even were our northern boundary absolutely settled.

Finally, I am persuaded that "winter roads" will in all probability be made before long by the enterprise of parties anxious to develop the resources of the territory This will result not only in the acquisition of further and more reliable information in reference to the importance and value of these resources, but also in regard to the best means of opening up the country generally, by colonization roads or otherwise.

EXPERIMENTAL FARMS.

In all the reports which I have had the honour to submit in reference to this territory, I have expressed the opinion that while the climate, in by far the greater portion of it, will admit of the growth of all the more important root and grain crops, the soil and other conditions are better suited to the breeding of store cattle and to dairy husbandry See Report for 1879-80, page 20 to 25, and Report for 1882-83, pp. 13, et seq.

To engage successfully in these latter branches of farming, it is not imperatively necessary that colonization or other roads should be made to each man's door. Store cattle can be driven many miles over a country which, if not already passable, can he rendered so with very little labour. The expense of driving cattle sixty or seventy miles to the nearest railway station or steam-boat landing is trifling. Nor would the transport of really good butter a like distance over winter roads be a very serious obstacle to the success of dairy farming, if the country and the climate were otherwise favourable. It a very different matter when the marketable produce of a country is grain or roots, even if that grain be wheat. Of this we have already sufficient evidence in the experience of settlers in the west and north-west.

If a portion of the money heretofore spent in promoting emigration were expended in placing beyond doubt the fitness of our northern territory for the growth of grain and root crops, and its particular adaptability for the raising of cattle and the making of cheese and butter, such an expenditure could not in my opinion fail to be the highest degree beneficial.

With this object in view I would respectfully suggest the establishment, at suitable points, of Experimental Farms in this territory.

The object sought to be obtained is not of the nature of "Model Farming," nor is the raising of large crops. That which we really want to find out is, what kind of crop can be raised in different parts of the territory? And further, in regard to those crop that will grow. Which are best adapted to the soil and climate, or, in other words, a most thrifty and productive? It is of vital importance, as bearing on the value of the territory, and the manner in which it should be opened up and developed, that the Government should know from actual experiment whether wheat, barley, oats, rye, pea beans, vetches, etc., will grow and come to maturity. As regards wheat again, wheth

. reliable crop in a territory like this, where the ground is covered
the entire winter? That potatoes grow well from the Height of
of James' Bay, has been sufficiently proved at the Hudson Bay
. there are other roots of no little importance, such as the carrot,
1 respect of which it would be desirable to have further informa-
.g on the suitability and value of the country for stock-raising and
ould certainly be well to know from actual experiment, what
1e territory, such as red and white clover, timothy, ryegrass, etc.,
e valuable for fodder, but for pasture also. It would be interest-
er the cultivation of flax, hemp and hops might be expected to be
of the smaller fruits even might be worthy of notice.
appears to me might be ascertained by carefully conducted experi-
1nd or less, and in a period of four or five years at the most. The
ite as satisfactory or reliable as those obtained by farming in the
1evertheless I think be exceedingly valuable to the Government
ince.
vould then have not merely opinions and reports, but reli ible facts
licy in regard to the opening up and development of the territory.
1at kind or class of settlers would be almost, if not quite, certain to
comfortable homes in the territory, and these and no others should
3re. The success and contentment of the first pioneers is the
1nd the surest way to people this or any other territory.
.hat these "Experimental Farms" will be too costly, but most of
1 reality more nearly resemble those of the "Market Gardener"
No expensive buildings need be erected, and those absolutely
:ructed of logs which can be easily procured on the spot. I believe
1ly located and properly handled, would be self-sustaining after the
o part of the capital invested need be lost. And further, that
1s the expense will be altogether trifling as compared with the
f the results.

OUR FUR-BEARING ANIMALS.

:ipal product of the Basin of Hudson's Bay has been furs. Other
's, oil, timber, fish and minerals have been comparatively of little

Company has been primarily and almost exclusively a fur-trading
ort has been made to develop other industries. To have drawn
agricultural or other resources of a territory in which they desired
1 of the fur trade, would have been suicidal.
the furs obtained in the Dominion of Canada, according to the
1, vol. 3rd, p. 249, was $987,555. This, I have reason to believe,
value. Indeed, it is simply impossible for census officers to obtain
ith respect to a matter of this kind, as to get from each hunter a
1t by him during the preceding year was thoroughly impracticable.
Hudson's Bay Company of 27th June, 1882, it would appear that
1d other imports into Great Britain, the returns of the outfit of
g freight, dock charges, cartage, fire insurance, etc., amounted to
ling, or $1,160,388 Canadian currency showing the value of the
udson's Bay Company alone to have been $172,833 more than that
urns for the whole of the Dominion. I am aware that included
1udson's Bay Company there are a few other things besides furs,
e oil, and feathers. But the amount of these is, I think. incon-
1ly more than covered by the thirty thousand dollars' worth of furs
r to the same year or "Outfit" said to be "in transit" at the time
1nd which appears as a separate entry in the accounts. I am also

aware that of the fur obtained by other traders in the Dominion, more or less is pur chased by the Hudson's Bay Company, and included in the proceeds of their London sales. But making every allowance for such purchases, the value of the furs obtained by others than the Hudson's Bay Company, and either retained for their own use or sold to the furriers and hatters in Canada and United States, is a very considerable item. Again, the proceeds of the furs of the Hudson's Bay Company for 1880-81, owing to the lowness of the prices obtained for some of the more important was, I believe, less than the average amount usually realized for the year's catch.

Altogether I feel justified in saying that the annual value of the furs obtained in the Dominion is not in all probability less than one and a-half millions of dollars. Of this million and a-half of dollars' worth of furs, probably from one-fourth to one-fifth part, or from three hundred thousand to four hundred thousand dollars' worth, are obtained from the Basin of Hudson's Bay proper. By the term "Basin of Hudson's Bay proper" I would be understood to mean the territory the water of which drains directly only into Hudson's Bay, to the exclusion of that part which drains primarily into Lake Winnipeg, and which in every respect, save that of the final drainage of its waters, via Nelson River, into Hudson's Bay, may be regarded as a distinct and separate Basin, forming the Upper or northern extremity of the great Mississippi valley.

If I were to say that the fur-bearing animals abounded throughout the whole of this territory, it would be indulging in a figure of speech at the expense of the truth. So far as my knowledge and experience enable me to form an opinion, the fur-bearing animals are really few in number as compared with the vast extent of the territory they occupy. In some districts this may be owing to the fact of their having been almost exterminated by the hunter and trapper. In others it is due to the nature of the country, those parts more especially which are overspread with peat-mosses, affording little food or shelter for animals of any kind. The possibility of obtaining food sufficient to sustain life limits absolutely not only the number of the fur-bearing animals but of every living thing. This food, too, must be procurable at stated intervals or as often as is required for the healthy existence of the creature. Some animals must have food almost hourly, others daily, and comparatively few can, I apprehend, survive any great length of time if the intervals be much more than twenty-four hours.

It follows from this law of Nature that the number of those animals which do not migrate is limited by the amount of food obtainable, not in the summer and autumn, when there may be over-abundance, but in the winter which is the season of scarcity. We have only to consider the length and severity of the winter in this country, the depth of the snow and frozen state of the ground, to understand in some measure how difficult it must be for animals of any kind to live through that season. In order to do so at all they must be specially adapted to the conditions of existence.

The larger herbivorous animals are confined to a very few species. Among these we find the caribou or rein deer, the moose-deer, the beaver, the ground-hog, the porcupine, the hare or rabbit, the musquash or musk-rat, the squirrel, and though not large yet numerous, mice of several kinds. Some of these lay up stores of food during the autumn, sufficient, with the fat on their backs, to see them through the winter. Others hybernate through the greater part of that season. The remaining animals are so organized as to be able to obtain food during the winter on which they manage to live. With the exception of the beaver and the musk-rat, however, nearly all the fur-bearing animals of the north are carnivorous, subsisting during the winter at least, almost entirely on fish or the flesh of other animals. Even the musk-rat will eat fresh water muscles and probably crawfish.

It may naturally be asked, What animals supply the vast quantity of meat (flesh) necessary for the subsistence of all the carnivorous fur-bearing animals in this territory? In reply to this I may say, that the mice are the main-stay of the ermine and must constitute no inconsiderable item in the food supply of the marten, the fisher and the fox, particularly when rabbits are scarce. There is little doubt, however, that in ordinary years the rabbit is the food on which the fisher, fox, lynx, and in many instances the Indians themselves, chiefly subsist during the winter. The winter food of the rabbit (the young shoots of the birch, aspen, etc.) is abundant almost everywhere, excepting on the muskegs, and is most easily obtained when the snow is deepest. The weight of this creature (about 3½ lbs.) is so small in proportion to the spread of its feet, that it can run with ease and rapidity on the surface of snow too soft to bear up, almost any other animal. It is thus enabled to obtain its food readily, and the deeper the snow the more of this food is brought within its reach. If the number of rabbits bore a steady proportion to the abundance of its food, the number of fur-bearing animals and of Indians also would no doubt be much greater than they are. Unfortunately, however, this rabbit, or more properly hare, so admirably adapted to the conditions of existence in other respects, is subject to epidemics by which it is periodically almost exterminated. The Indians generally suffer more or less at these times, and not a few actually die of hunger. It is natural therefore to conclude that great numbers of the fur-bearing animals, chiefly dependent on the rabbit for sustenance, must likewise perish.

The food of the otter and mink is less precarious, consisting as it does largely of fish which are found in all the lakes and rivers. The otter it is said will prey on young beaver, and the mink will undoubtaly kill and devour the musk rat and any of the smaller animals and birds that may come in his way. Both these animals are valuable for their fur, and would be much more numerous were they not too often shot when out of season, or so kept down by trappers that too few of the old ones are left to keep up the stock.

There is no fur-bearing animal in the north nearly so valuable as the Beaver, and none whose food is nearly so abundant at all seasons of the year. The value of the beaver-skins obtained in the territory owned by Ontario, exceeds in my opinion that of all the other furs put together. And in addition to the fur the meat of the beaver is wholesome and good. Its food consists of the bark, young shoots and branches of deciduous trees, with the roots of various aquatic plants. Trees of the pine species it does not like, if indeed it will touch them at all, save perhaps for the purpose of making its dams. Aspen, poplar, birch, willow and alder, furnish its favourite food, and these are found growing in practically unlimited quantity, on the banks of all the rivers, streams and lakes between our great lakes and James' Bay. It is said that the number of beaver is not decreasing north of the Height of Land, while south of the water-shed they are rapidly disappearing. It may be that there has been no diminution in their numbers north of the Height of Land within the last twenty or thirty years, but I am convinced that beaver must at one time have been much more numerous than now. One thing is absolutely certain, namely, that this increase is not limited by any insufficiency of food at any season of the year.

What the beaver really requires is protection against its enemies, and chiefly against the ignorance, improvidence and folly of man himself. Even when the fur is out of season and of comparatively little value, the Indians are irresistibly tempted to kill them for the food they afford. If the female be caught or shot in the early summer months, the young, four or five in number, necessarily perish. They die either for want of food or fall a prey to their enemies. Again, the beaver-dam is in my opinion not only necessary to enable these creatures to obtain and store up food for their winter use, but also to afford them protection against their enemies and the violent floods of mingled water and ice which pour down all the larger rivers in the spring. The inconsiderate and reckless destruction of these dams in order in some measure to facilitate the capture of the beaver is I believe a fatal mistake, and one of the principal causes of their decrease. The dams broken down and the water let off, those that escape seek temporary safety in the larger rivers. Here the old beaver may be able to survive for a time, but any lodges they may build must be completely submerged, or entirely swept away by the ice and water at the time of the spring freshet. If not crushed and killed, the young beaver are thus deprived of all shelter and protection, and fall an easy prey to their many enemies.

DOMESTICATION OF THE BEAVER.

The origin of our common domestic animals would seem to be hidden in the obscurity which overhangs the early history of our own race. The horse, ox, sheep, goat, pig and dog, have come to us as an inestimable legacy from pre-historic men of whom we know little or nothing. This much, however, we may be sure of, it was only after very much pains-taking and trouble on the part of these early benefactors of mankind, and this continued for many generations, that these animals were in the first instance tamed, and their nature so thoroughly changed, as to render them not merely useful, but absolutely necessary to the very existence of the far greater number of their descendants in subsequent ages.

It is somewhat strange that during the many centuries which have elapsed since the dawn of history, no new species of any great importance would appear to have been added to the domesticated animals then known. Admitting that these embrace *all* the animals of the Old World which were likely to be of any great use or advantage to mankind then or now, it is nevertheless singular that of those found in America and Australia none should have been thought worthy of domestication. While the greatest attention has been paid (this century more particularly) to the improvement of our existing stock of domestic animals, and with marvellous success, I am not aware of any persistent and well-directed effort in any quarter, the object of which is to add new and valuable species to the animals already domesticated.

Every one who has had the most limited experience in the country knows that the chief drawback to the more successful raising of sheep, cattle and horses, etc., in the whole of the northern part of this Continent, is the length and severity of the winter. It is needless to deny the fact that the necessity we are under of housing and feeding all the domestic animals that are kept in this country, for a period of five months in the year, is attended not only with a great deal of labour but a very great deal of expense. The mildness of the winters being such as to render the housing and feeding of cattle unnecessary, is the one great advantage which the breeders of sheep, cattle and horses, in Australia, South America and Texas, have over us. It is questionable if the summer pasture is nearly so good as ours. Now, as we cannot greatly mitigate the severity or shorten the length of our winter, the only alternative left is to find, if possible, some other animals than horses and even sheep, which may be capable of providing themselves with food all the year round, and at the same time likely to prove fairly remunerative to those who afford them such care and protection as may be required. The beaver and the rein-deer appear to me the only animals presumably capable of fulfilling these conditions. The rein-deer, or caribou, can procure food at any season in many parts of the territory, and the domesticated rein-deer of Lapland or Northern Siberia will doubtless be introduced into the territory sooner or later, and that with more or less satisfactory results. The beaver, on the other hand, is endowed with such intelligence that it anticipates the needs of the winter, and with marvellous industry lays up during the summer and autumn a sufficient stock of food for all its wants. It also builds its own houses and repairs its own dams, thus doing for itself all, or nearly all, that, which the farmer finds so expensive and laborious to do in the wintering of our common domestic animals.

In the Province of Ontario are many million acres of land which spontaneously produce abundant crops of aspen, birch, poplar, alder, willows, and other trees, besides shrubs, aquatic plants and roots. These are valueless, or nearly so, as food for our common domestic animals. More than that, these trees and shrubs must be cut down and destroyed at great labour and expense before the land, which is then said to be "cleared," can be cultivated and seeded down with the view to obtaining the nutritious grasses, roots and grain required by such animals. This, of course, involves a further expense, and one that must be incurred year after year. In view of this fact, and of that previously referred to, namely, the length and severity of our Canadian winter, I have no hesitation in saying that the beaver more completely fulfils the conditions which would render its domestication desirable than any other animal whatever.

The beaver is the largest and most valuable representative of the order "Rodentia." These Rodents, or gnawers, may be well said to have been specially created with a view to obtaining their subsistence and nourishment from such trees, shrubs and plants as are the natural and inexhaustible growth of our northern territory. Thus food sufficient to maintain countless numbers of beaver can be obtained at no cost, and practically in as unlimited abundance as the grass of the prairies. The admirable fitness of this Rodent for obtaining its subsistence from this source is specially shown in the structure of its teeth. The form and strength of these, the distinguishing characteristic of the whole order, are such as enable the beaver to cut down trees from four to four and a-half feet in circumference, as I have myself frequently seen. Whichever way we may regard it, whether it be as an adaptation of the animal to the food, or of the food to the animal, or to whatever cause we may ascribe it, be it to direct creation or to natural selection, the fact remains entirely unaffected, namely, that as regards its food the beaver is perfectly adapted to the conditions of its existence, and that there is hardly a limit to the number which our northern territory is capable of sustaining.

Nor is the beaver less admirably adapted to withstand the vicissitudes of climate. Its fur, close and thick, retentive of the animal warmth within, and impervious to moisture from without, is an ample protection against cold and wet, such as none of our domestic animals, not even the sheep, possesses in like degree. The northerly range of the beaver is limited rather by the influence of the climate on its appropriate food than the effect of cold directly on the animal itself. My opinion is that they may be found, other conditions being favourable, as far north as the aspen, birch and alder grow in sufficient quantity to supply them with food. While the region in which the beaver is said to have existed on this continent extends southwards nearly to the Gulf of Mexico, it stretches northward, in all probability, to within a short distance only of the Arctic Ocean. It is sufficient, however, for our present purpose to know, beyond doubt, that the beaver is thoroughly adapted to the climate of the most northerly part of the territory belonging to the Province of Ontario.

One other question suggests itself in connection with this branch of the subject, namely, what are the natural enemies of the beaver in this territory, by which its numbers have been so kept down, as to be out of all proportion to the prodigious quantity of its appropriate food ? By the natives the otter is generally regarded as one of the worst enemies of the beaver, destroying chiefly the young ones. Wolves and wolverines are also represented as preying on the beaver, and I have little doubt that they do so in some districts. There are but few, however, of these beasts in the territory belonging to the Province of Ontario, north of the Height of Land. It is more than probable that the lynx, fisher and fox will kill and devour the young beaver whenever they can surprise them out of the water. The lynx, I am persuaded, could kill an old beaver on dry land. If in the struggle, however, the beaver succeeded in reaching the water, it would most likely turn the tables on its enemy, and drown him if he did not relinquish his hold. I have little doubt that the system of warfare pursued by most, if not all, of these enemies, excepting the otter, is to lie in wait until the beaver leaves the water and enters the forest to procure its food, and then pounce upon and overpower it. Among birds, the eagle and eagle-owl are the only ones there is any reason to suppose powerful enough to prey on the beaver. While these animals and birds of prey doubtless destroy a great many beaver, it is nevertheless certain that the increase not only of the beaver, but of its enemies also, is checked and limited in a great measure by the number and activity of the Indian hunters and trappers. Provided by the trader with weapons and traps which the untutored savage could himself never have invented or made, the Indian wages a cruel and relentless war of destruction against every other living creature in the territory. So strong in him is the propensity to destroy life, and so overwhelming the desire to gratify it, that no consideration of mercy or of prudence can restrain him. It is rather due to the limitation of his own numbers, and consequent inability to utterly destroy than to any other cause, that the fur-bearing animals, at all events, have not been totally exterminated.

As bearing on the domestication of the beaver, it would be quite as easy, and more so, to protect the domesticated beaver against the depredations of its natural enemies, as the sheep.

With the view to forming a correct estimate of the probable value and importance of the beaver, supposing it to be capable of domestication, the following facts may be interesting :—

Beaver pair when about a year and a-half old, and the first litter is produced when the female is two years of age. They have only one litter in the year. This is brought forth in the month of May, and consists of from two to as many as seven or eight. Four young ones at a birth may be safely assumed to be the average. They do not attain full maturity until two and a-half or three years old. The weight of a full-grown beaver is a point on which my informants have differed materially; from thirty to sixty pounds would appear to be about the extremes.

The beaver has a two-fold value. Its fur is valuable, as everyone knows, made up into various articles of clothing, and its flesh is valuable as food.

The value of a full-grown beaver-skin was three and a-half dollars last spring on Lake Huron. The price, like that of every other product, whether of the forest or the field, varies not only according to the quality of the fur but with the demand. As the population and wealth of this continent increase, there can hardly fail to be a corresponding increase in the demand for the fur of the beaver, its beauty and warmth alike commending it to general favour.

The flesh of the beaver is wholesome, moderately nutritious, and much liked by those who have been in the habit of using it. It is not, in my opinion, inferior to the hare in any of these respects. I need hardly remark that both belong to the same order of animals, and that the beaver is quite as cleanly in its habits and in the choice of its food as the hare, rabbit or any other of the animals commonly made use of by man. In answer to a question as to how many rabbits would be equal to an ordinary sized beaver in respect of food, one of my voyageurs assured me that a beaver would afford as much food (nourishment) as thirty rabbits. As he had lived the greater part of his life on rabbits and beaver, and was upwards of fifty years of age, I feel a good deal of confidence in his judgment on this point. I know from observations made by myself many years ago, that the quantity of actual meat afforded by the rabbits on the north shore varies from one and a half to two pounds each, and think we may safely assume the meat on an average sized full-grown beaver to be not less than from thirty to forty pounds, and its value as food at least one dollar and a half. Thus estimated, the value of the whole animal will be five dollars, or as much as a sheep was worth not many years ago. But in an enquiry of this nature, it is proper to bear in mind the fact that it is not merely possible, but highly probable, that the value of the beaver may be greatly increased under domestication. If we only consider for a moment what the effects of domestication have been as regards the horse, the ox, the sheep, the pig, the dog, and in fact all our domestic animals and birds, the differences in size, in form, in colour and instincts, not only as compared with the the primitive or wild animal, but as compared with each other, we cannot come to any other conclusion than that like interesting and profitable variations may be obtained in the case of the beaver.

Every breeder of fine stock, or of animals of any kind, is perfectly aware of the important changes that can be effected in these respects by a judicious selection of the animals from which they breed. If this principle of selection be intelligently carried out in the domestication and breeding of the beaver, equally important and valuable results may be reasonably anticipated. It is not only possible but highly probable that these animals may be thus greatly increased in size and weight. I have already stated that the weight of a full-grown beaver usually varies from thirty to sixty pounds, and may even exceed sixty pounds in very exceptional cases. There is nothing therefore I think extravagant in the belief that by careful selection and breeding the size of the beaver may be increased to almost one hundred pounds. Nor is there anything unreasonable in the expectation that the larger quantity of meat might by some attention to the food be very much improved in quality. Then, as regards the fur, not only would the increased size of the skin obtained from the larger animal add materially to its value, but much might be expected from the different colours which it may be possible to obtain by judicious selection in breeding. This power to vary the colour is rendered more likely by the fact that although the colour of the beaver in the wild state is generally brown, the fur is not unfrequently nearly black, and I have been told that very light coloured beaver are not altogether unknown. I know this is the case with its closely allied species the musquash or muskrat, as I have seen skins which were nearly white.

It will doubtless appear strange and unaccountable to many, that an animal to which so much importance and value is attached in this report should not have been already domesticated. And this circumstance may be supposed to afford some grounds for thinking that the beaver is either not so valuable as represented, or that there may be some grea', if not insuperable, difficulty in respect of its domestication. Now, as regards the probable importance and value of the beaver to the future inhabitants of our northern territory, the facts I have adduced must speak for themselves. As regards the second point, a few words may not be out of place. The beaver appears to be easily tamed, and the Indians sometimes keep the young ones as pets for months; but I have never yet seen a full grown beaver that was so kept. There are several good reasons for this : such as, the wandering life which the Indian leads, the number of dogs which he keeps, and the temptation he is under to kill and eat the beaver whenever he has nothing for dinner, a very common occurrence in his experience. But the principal reason that neither the Indian or any other savage or even semi-civilized race has been able to keep and domesticate the beaver is, in my opinion, this :—In order to be of any utility or advantage whatever to man, the beaver, like other domestic animals, must be able itself to procure food, water, and other necessaries within certain prescribed limits, beyond which it cannot be permitted to go. In other words, it must be confined in an enclosure, from which it cannot, even if so disposed, possibly escape. Now, in view of the extraordinary instincts and intelligence of this animal, and the instruments with which Nature has provided it, no savage race of men could keep beaver thus confined. No fence that they could make would keep the beaver within such an enclosure as would be required. A ditch would be utterly useless. A wooden fence of any description, he could cut his way through without difficulty. A rude mason himself, I doubt if a dry-stone wall would keep him in, unless it was very carefully built. Indeed it is on the question of our own ability to construct, *at moderate expense*, a fence which the beaver can neither break through, burrow under, or crawl over, that the successful domestication and breeding of the beaver really depends. If, at moderate expense, such a fence can be made, success is, I believe, attainable, but not otherwise. A wire fence, specially designed or manufactured for the purpose, would, I feel persuaded, answer the purpose, and overcome, in all probability, this hitherto insuperable difficulty. It is possible that, when thoroughly domesticated, comparatively little restraint in the shape of fences may be needed, but undoubtedly this will be absolutely necessary for many years, if not many generations (of beaver), to come.

It is not pretended that the beaver can, or will, take rank with the horse, cow, sheep or pig in general usefulness and value to mankind, but I do claim that, to many of the future inhabitants of our northern and western territory, the raising of beaver may prove one of the most pleasant and profitable occupations in which they can possibly engage. One very important point in favour of the domestication and breeding of beaver is the ease and comparative cheapness with which its most valuable product, "fur," can be transported from the most remote and isolated parts of the territory to markets, however distant. A cost for transportation of five cents per pound, or five dollars per hundred pounds, would be an insuperable obstacle to the profitable raising of any sort of agricultural produce whatever. But this apparently exorbitant cost really counts for very little, when the value of the article produced is two or three dollars a pound, or from two hundred dollars to three hundred dollars per hundred pounds weight, as in the case before us.

I have never heard of any systematic attempt having been made anywhere, or by any person, to domesticate the beaver. I am aware that in Scotland, the Marquis of Bute had, some years ago, a number of beaver on the island of that name. But what may have been the object of his lordship in thus keeping them, I do not know. As our American wild turkey is also to be found on this nobleman's property, it is more than probable that both the beaver and turkey are kept rather as affording objects of interest to himself, his friends, and the public, than with any view to their domestication.

I have gone thus fully into this subject, rather in the hope of calling public attention to it, than in the expectation that the Government will undertake this experiment. But should private individuals or companies be induced to attempt "the domestication of the beaver," they should receive every reasonable assistance and encouragement from the Government.

PLEA ON BEHALF OF THE FUR-BEARING ANIMALS.

While on this subject, I earnestly desire to say a few words on behalf of the po
fur-bearing animals, whose lives are ruthlessly taken by hundreds of thousands to prom
the comfort or sometimes to gratify the pride and vanity only of mankind.

It would be out of place here, and it is therefore not my intention, to question t
morality of destroying great numbers of (in some instances) perfectly inoffensive a
harmless creatures, merely to gratify a whim, or in deference to some silly fashion.
What I desire to urge on their behalf is simply this, that if doomed thus to die,
obedience to the laws of their Creator, let their death, at all events, be as speedy and pa
less as possible; let substitutes be found for some of the cruel implements hitherto ig
rantly and thoughtlessly employed for their capture and destruction, but more especia
for "the steel trap."

Amid the many inestimable blessings and the many useful engines, tools and inst
ments that we have inherited from our ancestors in the old land, there are not wanti
some things, here and there, of which it may be said with at least apparent truth, that
the interests of humanity, it had been better the author or inventor had never been bo
One of these exceptionably evil things is "the steel trap," than which no fiendish inst
ment of torture ever devised by human ingenuity, even when inspired by the deadli
hate and directed solely to that horrible end, has been so fraught with indescribable p
and suffering to millions of our humbler and weaker fellow-creatures. Who this invent
this pitiless man, was; his name, country and race are alike unknown. There is har
a boy in England, however, who does not know what a steel-trap is, so universally are tl
employed for catching rats, and also for the destruction of cats, fitchets, weasles and ot
so-called "vermin" of the gamekeeper. There are few, perhaps, in this country outs
our towns and cities who do not know something at least of these traps. But for
information of those who may not fully understand their nature, a few words of expla
tion may not be altogether out of place.

The idea which led to the invention of the steel-trap has probably been sugges
by the structure of the mouths of beasts of prey. This is shown even in the names
ployed to designate its more important parts. It consists essentially of two powe
iron jaws, of the same size and shape, both resembling the lower jaws of a wild beast.
some traps these jaws are serrated or made with saw-like teeth; in some, hideous i
spikes are also placed at short intervals to represent the canine teeth; in others, and 1
generally in this country, there are no teeth, excepting in traps of the very largest s
In all, the opposing jaws meet or clench when shut, as in the beast of prey. These j
are hinged or jointed into an iron frame, and closed by one, and in the larger traps by 1
powerful steel springs. These springs correspond to and do the work of the "flex
muscles of the carnivorous animal. Within the jaws, when extended and lying with
teeth (if any) upward, is situated the "tongue," a thin iron plate or disk, situated al
the centre and partly filling the space encircled by the jaws. When the trap is "
this "tongue" is so adjusted that the lightest pressure of the foot of any animal ca
it to "go off," or, in other words, these dreadful iron jaws are brought together wi
quick and cruel snap, the force of which depends upon the size of the trap and stre
of the steel springs. But the force is at any rate such as frequently to fracture
sometimes completely smash the bones of the legs of the smaller animals.

The trapper sets these terrible steel traps at what he deems the most likely pl
guided by signs with which he is familiar. The size and strength of the trap is regul
by those of the animal he expects to catch. Some are baited with such food as experi
has taught him will be most tempting to the hungry creatures. Others are set in
paths or runs. Some at the entrance to their burrows or lodges. Others again (a
the otter), are not unfrequently set under water. All are as carefully hidden or
cealed as possible. These traps are arranged in lines, taking in a large extent of cou
around the trapper's camp. Thus scattered, some of these traps are often as mu
eight or ten miles from the camp, and that in opposite directions. It is not pos
therefore, for the trapper to visit his traps daily. In point of fact he rarely does

33

o or three days, and frequently from indolence, indisposition or iod that elapses between his visits *is very much longer.*
p killed its victims instantly nothing could be alleged against its h equal propriety be urged against the employment of any trap .r or like purposes of destruction, but with rare exceptions, and ller animals, the steel-trap does not kill its victims. As already most always by their legs, and the powerful snap of its cruel led with teeth or fangs) is often such as to fracture and occasion-s. It has also been shown that these steel-traps, when numerous ʒe tract of country, cannot be visited by the trapper at shorter iree days, and that these periods may be extended to a week I ask, must be the sufferings of these poor creatures during ιys and nights they are thus doomed to pass waiting for death ? e, four or five days, the thoughtless, if not callous and unfeeling, d misery condescends to put in a tardy appearance on the scene, ɔmetimes dead, sometimes dying, and at others in a stupified or mpled and blood-stained snow, the torn and broken bushes, often ιnd prolonged but vain struggle for freedom and for life, but even aving been broken or fractured, no force that the creature could e limb from the relentless and more than bull-dog grip of the ιews, bruised flesh and skin hold out, the wretched captive must eath puts an end to its misery.
f the fur-bearing animals, I am told, such as the otter, the fisher prevented, frequently amputate their legs with their teeth and maimed. Even the poor, industrious and harmless beaver, perhaps ιntelligence, will sometimes, either by twisting the fractured limb cin alike give way, or by the actual use of its teeth, free itself ɘgain its liberty.
o frequent and too true, to require that the picture should in the drawn or exaggerated, in order to enlist the sympathy of the . Nor would it be right to omit notice of the fact, that at fault his self-interest is sometimes made to supply the want. ɔre us, the skins of such fur-bearing animals as escape out of his ιpper, his ingenuity has been stimulated to devise means whereby rtunately for the beaver and the otter, the means adopted by generally puts a speedy end to their sufferings, and in this way : ch these animals are commonly set either a little below the surface anks of some river or lake. Knowing that their first impulse, ɪlunge into the water, the trapper allows as much chain as he can ι stone to it near the trap, if the weight of the trap and chain icient for the purpose. The other end of the chain is, of course, ɔank.
nple arrangement will be easily understood. The creature, in its to escape, plunges into the water, is sunk to the bottom by the chain, and stone, and soon drowned. Thus, as a rule, ιver and the otter are not very protracted. But, to this rule, exceptions, entailing on them all the agonies I have endeavoured g-pole," which is used in connection with the traps set for the that when the creature is caught and strains on the chain of the . and hoists both the trap aud its victim several feet from the ɘd in mid-air, by its crushed and bruised, perhaps broken, leg, ιy writhe and struggle, but it cannot, I have been told, while in twist off its leg, and thus escape as it would otherwise do. How ; in this pitiable condition before death comes to its relief I am ɔo probable that it is many long hours. The spring-pole is also ιation with traps set for animals which when caught rarely escape, n the ground, might be torn or devoured by other carnivorous

animals, and the fur thus injured or lost entirely. Of this addition to the steel trap, all that can be said is that, while simple and efficient as a means of saving "the fur," it has little, if any, claim to our admiration as a contrivance which mitigates the sufferings of the poor fur-bearing animals.

I trust I have now said sufficient to obtain from the Government and the Legislature the favourable consideration of any measure which may be brought forward for an amelioration of the sufferings of these speechless and unrepresented denizens of our northern forests,

But much more than legislation is needed to (if I may be allowed to use that expression) remedy the wrongs and remove the evils under which they are labouring. Public sympathy must also be aroused.

It is true we have societies for the prevention of cruelty to animals. An object altogether praiseworthy, and presenting a field so large as to afford the most ample scope for the exercise of the kindly and benevolent feelings of its members. The sphere, however, of this society's labour is, I apprehend, confined chiefly, if not entirely, to domesticated animals.

Again, there are societies whose aim is the suppression of the practice of vivisection as a special and unjustifiable form of cruelty to animals. In comparison with the suffering of the fur-bearing animals, and of cats and rats, from the use of the steel-trap, that o the few creatures subjected to vivisection is so trifling, numerically and in intensity, as to be almost infinitesimal. I have not a doubt that, at this moment of writing, thousand upon thousands of poor creatures are struggling in the jaws of these fiendish and crue traps, and suffering all the agonies I have endeavoured so imperfectly to describe.

It is unfortunate that, for the capture of many kinds of wild animals, and even bird of prey, this trap is unequalled.

The "dead-fall" and "the snare," probably known to, and used by, the Indians an other savage races from the earliest times, are equal, if not superior, to the steel-trap i the capture of several of the fur-bearing animals, and happily they are still generall employed for that purpose. In simplicity and in point of humanity these methods ar as nearly perfect as they can be. Both kill almost instantly, the one by crushing, th other by strangulation, and the death of the creatures thus caught is "as speedy an painless as possible." They fairly fulfil, in my opinion, the moral requirements of th situation, as stated in the first part of this plea. They are employed chiefly in the captu of the marten, always for catching the hare or rabbit, and to some extent for the bea the lynx, the mink, and the fisher.

The steel-trap, on the other hand, is principally, if not entirely, used in catching tl wolf, fox, beaver, otter, ermine, and musk-rat, and partly employed in catching a the other animals, with the exception of the hare.

Now, so long as the steel-trap excels all other traps in efficiency in the capture of ar of these animals, neither legislation nor public opinion can possibly prevent its emplo ment by trappers. In addition to these restraining agencies, some substitute efficient, if not more so, than the steel-trap must, if possible, be provided, and one th is at the same time free from that revolting cruelty which renders the employment the steel-trap by any intelligent civilized man, even for the capture of rats or oth creatures which it is absolutely necessary to destroy, almost criminal.

I have entire faith in the ability of the mechanics of the present day to desi and make a trap or traps that will fulfil these conditions. Nay, more; traps tl will be superior in efficiency to the steel-trap, and at the same time confer on the doom creature, whose only crime has been that it was born and has tried to live according its instincts, that to which it is fairly entitled, a speedy and painless death.

In order thereto it may be necessary that liberal premiums should be offered stimulate mechanics and others to supply this want.

It is not expected that the Government should offer such premiums, but while Government, it is hoped, may see fit to favour the necessary legislation, the ventilat of the subject in this report and otherwise may move benevolent individuals, or societ such as that for "the Prevention of Cruelty to Animals," to take the matter up ı carry it to a successful issue.

isting on the moral obligations we are under to deal mercifully
reaker fellow-creatures, and that even in the mode and manner of
, becomes necessary to kill them, I must not be understood as
implication to fur-traders or trappers as a class, blame for the
uel disregard of the sufferings of the fur-bearing animals, which
that they themselves and their children may live. The fur-trade,
he principles of justice and equity, is as honourable as any other
if the trapper, followed as it might and should be, is not incom-
.er of an intelligent, honest, and even kind-hearted man. That
d is guilty of the atrocities which I have endeavoured to expose,
his fault. Others than he have been and are unwittingly guilty
rely to their fellow-creatures (the dumb animals so called), but to
rant, thoughtless, and more or less callous, he may be, but not
y and intentionally cruel.
I do, that the trapper shall abandon the use of the steel-trap and
ays of catching fur-bearing animals, is it my wish or intention
least. On the contrary, I fully believe that with his old time-
raps, the dead-fall, and the snare, and such other improved traps
supplied to him in place of the cruel steel-traps, he will be able
ing animals which his hunting-ground can produce. I would fain
her would be better off than now. For the practice of cruelty, even
he growth or renders callous some of the finest and best feelings
rrants the conclusion that the more humane and merciful the
e prosecution of his calling, the more rapid will be his progress,
ially, in civilization.

)N BEHALF OF THE NATIVES OF THE TERRITORY.

n of the natives was referred to at some length in my first report,
et seq. In this report I stated " that a large proportion of the
e more or less European blood in their veins." A more general
ation has confirmed this opinion. The European element is almost
and Scandinavian. There are very few French, Metis or Half-
It is almost impossible to tell what number of inhabitants there
of the territory north of the Height of Land, owned by our
on Census of 1882 was obtained by enumerating all the families
the Hudson Bay Company's Posts, and, as many of these were
ar the boundary, the population, as thus taken, included Indians
wn estimate, as given in the report for 1879-80, was 2,500, and
tion, " the treaty Indians," many of whom hunt during the winter
f the Height of Land. I still think that the population does not

ome of the Hudson Bay Company's Officers, with whom I have
t, the native population in this territory is not decreasing, but
some large families at Albany Factory, and elsewhere, I am
ves of the pure Indian race are not only decreasing, but must

nd inter-marriage with other races, all combine to that end.
h, and other epidemics, have carried off a great many within the
intercourse with the outside world becomes more frequent and
whiskey will each doubtless exact its quota of victims. The
have a medical officer on the staff at Moose Factory, but at no
tment.
h these diseases occasion is greatly aggravated by the want of
shelter, if not clothing, and of good nursing. A small hospital
ch needed and would save many lives.

A people depending so entirely on game and fish for their subsistence, somewhat improvident in making provision for the future, and with very inadequate means of preserving the surplus of food that may be obtainable at one season to meet the necessities of another, must frequently be reduced to the direst straits when game and fish fail. Indeed, with the exception of those employed as voyageurs and haymakers at the Hudson's Bay Company's Posts, and who for the time being are well fed, by far the greater proportion of the natives I meet with on my voyages look hungry and half famished. Even at the posts there are many hungry-looking women and children to be seen.

There are few Indian families, however, in the territory that do not now consume more or less flour, oatmeal, lard and pork, flour more particularly, of which some families will, notwithstanding its high price, use as much as four or five bags yearly.

Warm clothing and blankets are almost as indispensable as food during the winter season. The natives no doubt at one time clothed themselves in the bear, beaver and other skins that are now bartered or sold to the Hudson's Bay Company. The skins of the rabbit or hare are still to some extent made into garments and blankets. They are not, however, very durable and are only fit for dry-cold weather. Now, however, the natives have generally come to depend on the Hudson's Bay Company for blankets, capots and other articles of clothing. In fact everything the natives use in the way of food, flesh-meat excepted; everything in the way of clothes, with the exception of mocassins, and every single article they require for other purposes, such as axes, knives, guns, nets or twine, shot, powder, etc., is imported from Great Britain.

It is only since the Hudson's Bay Company sold their exclusive rights of trade, etc., to the Dominion that the natives and other inhabitants of this territory have been burdened with any customs duties. It will be easily understood, therefore, that the present high tariff, increasing as it does the price of all the necessaries of life, is exceedingly grievous to them.

It is the more keenly felt inasmuch as, although the sum of $100,000 at least has already been collected from them at the Port of Moose Factory alone, nothing whatever has been expended by the Dominion Government, whether for public works, postal facilities, support of schools, missions, medical attendance, or in any other form or way calculated to advance their comfort and welfare. In fact their closer connection with the Dominion of Canada, so far from resulting in any benefit to them, has been an unmitigated evil.

I believe that the Bishop of Moosonee (if not others) has made some representation on the subject of the grievances of the native population to the Premier and Minister o the Interior, but no action has been taken in reference thereto, that I know of.

Entirely isolated and cut off, as the people of this territory are, from all commercia intercourse with other parts of the Dominion, and deriving no benefit whatever from thei political connection with the Dominion, it is from every point of view unjust that the should be thus taxed. Heaven knows! the natives are poor enough, and suffer enoug from insufficient food and clothing; and the exaction of taxes from these people, amountin on an average to at least ten dollars per annum each family, is not only unjustifiable bu positively cruel.

The proper remedy for this injustice is to make Moose Factory and York Factor Free Ports, until connected by railway or otherwise with the rest of the Dominion. I may be objected that such a concession might lead to the smuggling of goods from thi territory into other parts of the Dominion, to the injury of the revenue, as was said t have been the case when (to encourage settlement) the Ports in Algoma and Gasp districts were declared "free." There is nothing, however, to support such an objectio A glance at the map will satisfy any unprejudiced person that the positions of the por on Hudson's Bay, and those in Gaspé and Algoma District, are totally different. A regards the first, the ocean freight is so high, and the difficulty and expense of transpo inland so enormous, that the idea goods so imported would be smuggled into the settl ments on the north shores of Lake Huron or Superior, or even into the North-West, absurd. Whereas, the running of such "free goods" from Gaspé into Quebec City, or fro Sault St. Marie into Collingwood or Owen's Sound, was a comparatively easy matter. Thu while smuggling in the one case might be exceedingly easy and profitable, it would in the other be exceedingly difficult and entail a ruinous loss on the smuggler.

If there be insuperable objections to making these free Ports, then unquestionably the amount of the duties thus collected should be expended or returned in such way and manner as will be most generally advantageous to those by whom the duties have been paid. That these duties have increased the cost of all the necessaries of life to the consumers, in this part of the Dominion at any rate, no one can possibly with the slightest show of reason deny, nor will any one have the temerity to assert that these customs duties have added anything to the value of the "furs" which are the only marketable product of the territory.

Nor is it by customs duties alone that the prices of the necessaries of life are rendered so dear. The cost of freight or transport, which adds greatly to the price of everything, is simply enormous in respect of some of the most important articles. For example, flour, lard and pork, if bought either in the United States or in Canada, must be sent first of all to London, then to Moose Factory, and thence inland by canoes or boats from one to three hundred miles.

Again, in view of the possibility of the loss or detention of their ships in Hudson's Straits or Bay, the Company must always keep a two years' supply of the most necessary articles at Moose and York Factories. This locks up a large amount of capital, the interest of which has also to be charged in the price to the consumer.

It is to be hoped, then, that the Dominion Government will not delay to take into favourable consideration the peculiar and altogether exceptional position of the Natives and others in this territory, and deal fairly, if not liberally, with them.

Christian philanthropy, which has done much to promote the spiritual welfare of the Natives of this territory, might have done also a great deal to promote their temporal welfare, comfort and happiness. The one has been the work of the Church Missionary Society of London, and of the Catholics of Quebec; the other should have been, it seems to me, the special care of the Hudson's Bay Company.

The servants of the Company, as distinguished from the hunters and trappers, are engaged for a term of years, at wages varying from twenty to thirty pounds a year, with a ration of food sufficient only for themselves. A few of the mechanics may get more, but the wages do not usually exceed that amount. Many of these are Scotchmen or Scotch half-breeds. As long as they remain unmarried they can live, and even save money. Few, however, do this; the far greater number marry Indian or half-breed women. The single ration, together with what the wife may be able to add by fishing and hunting, suffices the young couple for a while. But as child after child is born, the annual pittance of wages is drawn upon not only for clothing but for food. At the prices charged (and which it is to some extent necessary to charge) in this territory, the man's wages will not go very far. The quantity of game and fish at or near the Trading Posts is not great, nor at all times to be procured. And when the families are large and chiefly girls they are, I fear, very sorely pinched to live. If the father dies, their condition is still more pitiable. There is no employment for women, and as to getting out of the country to seek it elsewhere, it is simply impossible. It is a mystery to me how many of them do live. If some scheme could be devised to afford these and other poor women remunerative employment, it would greatly ameliorate and improve their condition.

One suggestion I may be permitted to make, and I do so in the hope that it may commend itself to favourable consideration.

A very large quantity of ready-made clothing is imported for the people in this territory, or for what is known as the Southern Department. The greater part, if not the whole, of this clothing could be, just as well if not better, made by the women at Moose Factory, Albany Factory, and Rupert's House, to whom such employment, at anything like reasonable and fair wages, would be one of the greatest of blessings. By the importation of the materials only, instead of the made-up or manufactured articles, a very considerable amount of duty would be saved.

All that is needed to carry out this scheme is an experienced foreman and a sufficient number of sewing machines. A foreman having a knowledge of cutting and fitting men's

4 (B. R.)

clothes, with a wife who had some knowledge of dress-making, would probably be the best combination.

So far from costing anything, I believe this suggestion, if carried out, would save the present importers a considerable sum of money. But even if it should not do so, and be only self-sustaining, the benefits that it could not fail to confer on a number of poor girls and women at the places referred to, should ensure its adoption.

If the natives could be induced to turn their attention to the cultivation of the soil, even if it were confined to the growth of potatoes, they would form an important addition to their supply of food. But peas and beans can be also grown in the greater part of the territory, and as food for the Indians these are not only exceedingly nutritive, but have over most other grains this advantage, that they can be used whole or unground, thus dispensing with the necessity for mills. The land thus cultivated should be on or near the hunting-ground of each family, in order that the food produced might be available, where and when, most required. The few simple instructions needed in reference to the choice of the land, and the planting of the seeds, might be very easily imparted at the missions or at the fur trading posts. If the Government supplied seed for a few years, the cost of which would be very trifling, I am persuaded that the Missionaries would willingly undertake to distribute it, and do all in their power to ensure, the success of any effort to ameliorate the condition of the natives in this or any other way.

The much needed assistance which the Provincial Government and Legislature would doubtless have given toward the support of schools in this territory has been lost ; and the administration of justice has been rendered all but impossible, by the refusal of the Dominion Government to admit the rights of our Province.

Respectfully submitted,

E. B. BORRON,
Stipendiary Magistrate.

www.ingramcontent.com/pod-product-compliance
Lightning Source LLC
Chambersburg PA
CBHW030914260626
47169CB00008B/2843

*9 7 8 3 3 3 7 1 2 5 4 8 6 *